"A

op W9-AUY-400

1208 S. Wayne St., Angola, IN 46703
260.665.1414

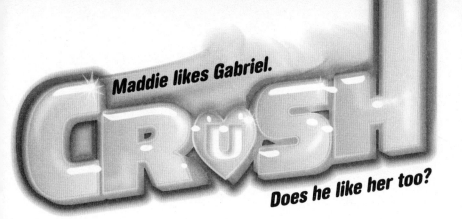

Maddie likes Gabriel.

Does he like her too?

Maddie's Camp Crush
by Angela Darling

SIMON SPOTLIGHT
New York   London   Toronto   Sydney   New Delhi

This book is a work of fiction. Any references to historical events, real people, or real places are used fictitiously. Other names, characters, places, and events are products of the author's imagination, and any resemblance to actual events or places or persons, living or dead, is entirely coincidental.

SIMON SPOTLIGHT
An imprint of Simon & Schuster Children's Publishing Division
1230 Avenue of the Americas, New York, New York 10020
Copyright © 2013 by Simon & Schuster, Inc.
Text by Tracey West
Designed by Dan Potash
SIMON SPOTLIGHT and colophon are registered trademarks of Simon & Schuster, Inc.
For information about special discounts for bulk purchases, please contact Simon & Schuster Special Sales at 1-866-506-1949 or business@simonandschuster.com.
Manufactured in the United States of America 0413 FFG
First Edition 10 9 8 7 6 5 4 3 2 1
ISBN 978-1-4424-8334-7 (pbk)
ISBN 978-1-4424-8335-4 (hc)
ISBN 978-1-4424-8336-1 (eBook)
Library of Congress Control Number 2012950723

chapter 1

"MOM, YOU WERE SUPPOSED TO TURN LEFT, NOT
right!" Maddie Jacobs said impatiently as her mother
turned down a lonely looking dirt road.

"Recalculating," announced the cool computer voice
of the GPS.

"See? I told you!" Maddie said.

Mrs. Jacobs brushed a strand of brown hair from her
face. "I'm just doing what the stupid machine told me
to, Maddie," her mom explained in a voice filled with
frustration.

"Actually, that is not what the stupid machine told you
to do," Maddie pointed out. "By the time we get to camp,
the season will be over!"

Her mother gripped the wheel. "Maddie, I'm doing
my best, okay? Just let me concentrate."

Maddie leaned back in her seat and resisted the urge

to make another comment. Mom had been such a mess since Maddie's father died in the fall. Losing Dad had been hard on everybody, but her mom just didn't seem to be getting any better. It sounded harsh, but sometimes Maddie wished she would just get it together already.

Sighing, Maddie turned to look out the window. Camp was an hour and a half away from home, in the woods of Pennsylvania. The roads were lined with green trees, and the sky above was a perfect July blue. But looking at the familiar scenery only made Maddie feel sad.

When Dad was alive, the trip to camp had been one of the most fun parts of the whole summer. Dad would sing songs that he'd learned at camp when he was a kid, and he'd roll down the windows and they'd all sing along with him loudly. Then he'd make corny jokes about camp, and even though he told the same ones every year, Maddie would still crack up.

"Why did the camper put a snake in the other camper's bed?" Dad would ask, and Maddie would pretend she didn't know the answer.

"Why?" she would say.

"Because she couldn't find a frog!" Dad would finish, and he and Maddie would laugh while her mom rolled her eyes—but she was always smiling.

Then when they got to camp, he would give Maddie the biggest, tightest good-bye hug ever, and he would even pretend to cry, making all her camp friends laugh. In truth Maddie was always a little sad when her parents left, but she never missed them for long because her dad always left a funny note hidden somewhere that Maddie would find—under her pillow or tucked in her slipper or even in the pocket of her bathrobe. Her throat tightened as she thought about the fact that there wouldn't be a note this year. She started to tear up, and she turned to the window to make sure her mom wouldn't see her.

After a deep breath, Maddie glanced at the clock. It was 11:03, and she started to feel anxious. Check-in had started an hour ago, and the girls who checked in first got to pick their beds first. If she didn't get to sleep near Liza, Libby, and Emily, her best camp friends, it would be terrible.

I'll probably end up with a bed next to the shower or the bathroom or something, she thought gloomily. Liza had said she would try to save her a bed, but they weren't supposed to do that, so Maddie was sure she'd be stuck. She wouldn't be surprised, considering how things had been going wrong ever since last night. After Maddie had packed her duffel bag with everything she needed for six weeks of summer camp, her mom realized that she couldn't lift it and drag it down the stairs to the car. That had never been a problem for Dad. He would always hoist it high over his head and say, "Oof, Mads, what did you pack, brick bathing suits?"

So this morning Mom had called Mr. Donalty from next door and he'd put the bag in the car for them. He was really nice about it, but the whole thing made Maddie miss her dad even more. Besides that, Mom had forgotten to make her special going-away breakfast. Dad had always made her French toast or pancakes.

"Eat up, Mads," he'd say. "You're going to be eating that icky camp food for weeks!"

All Mom had said this morning was, "Are you hungry?" Maddie had answered no, but Mom handed her a bagel as they left the house.

Now she snuck a look at her mother, who was leaning close to the steering wheel and gripping it tightly. She knew that Mom hated driving far from home, but she didn't accept Uncle Jay's offer to drive them up this year. Maddie wasn't sure why, but her Mom had been funny about accepting help from anyone lately.

Maddie's thoughts shifted to her camp friends, Liza and Libby and Emily. They'd come to the funeral last fall, but that whole thing was a blur. Maddie had been texting them all year long, but it wasn't the same as seeing them in person. She couldn't wait until they could all hang out together, laughing and talking like they always did. Just as long as they didn't want to talk about her dad. . . . She didn't care if Libby told that story about when the possum surprised her in the bathroom that one summer, even though Libby had told it a million times already. She'd rather talk about anything but her dad.

"Camp is going to be good for you, Maddie," her mom had said when Maddie had talked about skipping it this year. "It'll take your mind off things."

Maybe Mom was right, Maddie thought. The excitement of seeing her camp friends again was a really good feeling, a feeling she hadn't felt in a long time.

"Recalculating," announced the GPS again.

"*Mom!*" Maddie yelled, and her mother jumped in her seat.

"Don't yell while I am driving, Madeline!" she yelled back.

Maddie pouted quietly while her mom made another turn. Finally, Maddie saw the familiar sign down the road to the right: CAMP WIMOWAY ENTRANCE A.

"Finally!" Maddie cried, and a look of relief came over her mom's face as she turned down the narrow winding road to camp.

The tree-lined road emerged into a clearing of rustic wood cabins. Cars filled the parking lot as parents dropped off their campers, but Maddie didn't recognize any of them . . . because they were all boys!

Maddie and her mom exited the car, confused. A male counselor wearing a red Camp Wimoway shirt approached them.

"Here for drop off?" he asked.

"Yes," Mrs. Jacobs replied, anxiously looking around. "She's in the Hannah bunk this year."

Camp Wimoway was divided into a boys' camp and a girls' camp, and each camp was divided into bunks, or cabins. In the girls' camp the bunks were named after former counselors from a long time ago: Hannah, Sarah, Betty, and Gail.

"We've rearranged camp this year," the counselor informed them. "We sent out a map and a note, but some parents didn't get them, I'm afraid."

Mom looked a little guilty. *Great*, Maddie thought. *More changes.*

"You should have gone to Entrance B," the counselor explained. "It's about a quarter mile down the road and then you make a left." Mrs. Jacobs took a little notebook from her purse and he started to draw a map for her.

Maddie remembered that Entrance B led to the camp where the "baby" camp division was—the camp for kids who were, like, six to eight years old. And now that was where the girls' camp was? How embarrassing! Why couldn't Mom have read that e-mail? She started to slink back into the car before anyone noticed she was in the wrong place, but curiosity took over and she looked around at her old camp once more. It was weird to think that the boys were now living where the girls used to live.

A mom and dad walked past with a crying little boy, and Maddie knew how he felt. She had cried her first year in camp too. She looked at her cabin from last year and saw a couple of the boys her own age hanging around on the steps: Jared and Evan. They both looked so much taller than they were last summer! Then Brandon walked up to them. He lived only one town over from Maddie back home, and they had taken a tennis class together in the spring. He nodded at her, half-waving, and she looked away.

He's probably wondering why I'm standing in the middle of the boys' camp like a loser, she thought, and then she turned to open the car door, eager to become invisible before anyone else noticed her.

The sound of a voice coming from a nearby bunk made her pause. It was a boy's voice, a really cool, deep voice with a British accent. She turned slightly and saw a boy about her age—a boy with the most beautiful face she had ever seen.

chapter 2

MADDIE FOUND HERSELF JUST STARING AT THE
boy, something she had never done before. He had dark
hair and dark eyes and a few freckles across his cheeks.
He looked even taller than Jared and Evan, with long
arms and legs, like a swimmer. He was leaning against
the rail of the bunk looking exasperated as he talked to
a red-haired woman who Maddie guessed was his mom.

"Mum, I'll be just fine," he was saying. "I'll get along
swimmingly, I promise."

Swimmingly? Maddie cocked her head. Maybe he
was a swimmer—or was that some British term?

The boy's mom was weeping now, and dabbing her
eyes with a tissue. The boy looked like Maddie had felt a
few minutes ago—like he might die of embarrassment.

"Oh," his mother said, sniffing. "I know you'll have a
wonderful time, but I'll miss you so much!"

That's odd, Maddie thought, intrigued. *She talks like an American—no accent.*

Then the boy's mom hugged him tightly, and when he spotted Maddie looking at him, his face turned bright red. She froze—caught!—then smiled shyly and shrugged to show she understood how embarrassing parents can be. He grinned at her and rolled his eyes as he hugged his mother back.

"Okay, Mum, that's enough!" he said. "You ought to be getting along now!"

That only made his mom break out in a fresh round of tears. But Maddie didn't get to see how the boy's plight ended because her mom came back to the car.

"Okay, Madeline, I've got it now!" she yelled, waving the paper over her head. It was Maddie's turn to roll her eyes, and the boy laughed. Maddie grinned and shrugged again, and got into the car.

As they pulled away from the boys' camp, Maddie couldn't help looking back to get one last look at the boy. He was the cutest boy she'd ever seen—even cuter than that actor who played the werewolf in that movie. Way cuter, maybe because of the freckles, or the British accent; she couldn't decide.

She was lost in thought when her mom finally pulled up in front of the Hannah bunk in the girls' camp. Except for the carved wood sign above the door, which read HANNAH, it looked like the other bunks in camp: a simple wooden rectangular building with an open porch, screened windows, and white paint peeling from summers in the sun.

"*Maddie!*" a voice squealed.

Maddie hurried to get out of the car as her friend Liza Harry raced off the porch to greet her, jumping up and down and screaming. Liza hadn't changed much since last year; she was still two inches taller than Maddie, and her straight blond hair was pulled back in a blue headband. Like Maddie, she wore a red Camp Wimoway T-shirt and shorts, only Maddie's were black and Liza's were light blue, her favorite color.

"I've been here for *hours* already!" Liza said, practically dragging her up the cabin steps.

"Well, yeah, my mom kind of got lost," Maddie muttered.

A young woman in her twenties came out of the bunk. Her camp T-shirt read COUNSELOR across the front and back, and her black hair was braided into dozens of thin, tight braids and then wrapped into a ponytail.

"I'm Tara," she said, smiling at Maddie, and then she extended a hand to Mrs. Jacobs. "I'll be Maddie's counselor this summer."

"Nice to meet you," Maddie's mom said. "Um, do you think you could please help me get Maddie's duffel out of the car?"

"No problem," Tara said with a grin, and she headed to the car as Liza pulled Maddie inside the cabin.

The room erupted into happy shrieks as Maddie's friends Libby and Emily ran up to her.

"Oh my gosh, Maddie, I love your haircut!" Libby shrieked.

Maddie's brown hair had always hung halfway down her back, but getting the tangles out was always a chore. After Dad had . . . well, she decided on a change. Her hair wasn't short, exactly, it was more medium length, but she liked the way it swung against her shoulders now.

"Yours too," Maddie said. Libby always had her thick, glossy black hair styled in some new way. This year was a straight bob with really cute bangs.

"Thanks," Libby replied. "I don't know how long it's

going to last, though. The bangs get in the way when I play tennis."

"You should just cut all your hair off then," chimed in Emily. "And dye it bright yellow, like a tennis ball."

"Gross!" Libby squealed, and Emily's green eyes looked slightly hurt behind her glasses.

"I was serious," Emily said. "That would be cool!"

"Coming through!"

Tara and Mrs. Jacobs came through the door, each carrying one side of Maddie's enormous duffel bag.

"Over here, Mrs. J," Liza said, motioning to the second bed from the door. The main room of the cabin was sparse, with three bunk beds jutting out from opposite walls, and a small dresser next to each one. Along the back wall there were shelves where each girl could keep her clothes.

Liza leaned over to Maddie and whispered to her, "Tara let me save a bed for you. She's pretty cool."

Grateful, Maddie went to open her bag but her mom held up a hand.

"I'll unpack," she said. "You spend some time with your friends."

Maddie didn't argue. Mom always loved to fold her

underwear into tiny, neat squares. Maddie always thought it somehow helped her deal with the idea of saying good-bye for a whole summer. Like if Maddie's shelves were neat, everything would turn out fine.

Maddie turned back to her friends to see Emily standing next to a girl Maddie hadn't seen before.

"Maddie, this is Samantha," Emily announced.

"Nice to meet you," Samantha said shyly.

"Is this your first time at camp?" Maddie asked.

Samantha nodded. "Yeah, it's a little weird."

"Only Emily is a little weird," Liza told her. "The rest of us are fine."

"What can I say? It's true," Emily said, and everyone laughed.

It felt so good to Maddie to be talking and joking around—better than she'd felt in a really long time. She was surrounded by friends and it felt good to be away from home, where it seemed like a gray cloud had hung over everything since her dad died. At home, people still talked in soft voices and always asked her, "Is everything okay?" with sad eyes. Here, in camp, things finally felt normal again.

The girls were talking a mile a minute, and all at once.

Liza told her about the new pool at camp. Libby complained about the mandatory swim instruction that had been worked into the daily camp schedule. Emily was kind of mad that the boys got the girls' old camp.

As they talked, a girl with long, light-brown hair and blue eyes breezed into the cabin, trailed by a man carrying five bags of luggage.

"So, they said I could pick my own bed," the girl announced when she came in, and then she just kind of stood there, like she was waiting for something.

"Well, we all got here first, so that's the only one left," Liza said, pointing to the third bed on the right wall. "I'm Liza, and this is Libby and Emily and Maddie and Samantha."

The girl didn't introduce herself. "Oh," she said, not moving. "I think there's been some mistake. I was supposed to be able to pick my own bed. Dad?"

Her father shrugged helplessly, but just then Tara walked up and gave the girl a big smile. "You must be Amelia," she said, and then nodded to Amelia's father. "Follow me, and I'll make sure you settle in just fine."

Maddie and her friends exchanged glances. Every year, there always seemed to be one difficult camper. Was Amelia going to be the one?

"Oh, I almost forgot!" Libby said. "I have the best news. I'm going to be staying for the whole summer this year, and so is Emily."

"Really? No way!" Maddie squealed happily, hugging both of them. Every year, camp lasted for two three-week sessions from July to August. And every year, all of Maddie's friends had to leave after the first three weeks, leaving Maddie alone with the new campers.

When the girls stopped celebrating, Maddie noticed that Liza looked a little bit sad.

"I wish you could stay too," Maddie told her.

"Me too," Liza said glumly. "But you know how it is. I have to go on that family vacation to see my boring cousins in California every year."

Maddie nodded sympathetically. "It stinks, I know."

Then Maddie noticed that her mom had pulled Tara into a corner and was intently whispering to her. Tara had a look of concern on her face.

Oh great, Maddie thought. *She's probably telling her how Dad died, and now Tara and everyone else around here is going to be whispering and giving me the sad look.*

Then Maddie's mom saw her watching them and broke away from Tara.

"Okay, Madeline," her mom said. "Time for me to get out of here."

Maddie was surprised to feel a well of sadness rise up inside her. Sure, she had cried when she was a kid, but the last few years the first day of camp had been easy because she knew she was going to have so much fun.

Maddie followed her mom outside. "What if you get lost again?" Maddie asked, suddenly worried. "And what will you do in the house all by yourself for six weeks? Six weeks!" Suddenly it felt like an eternity.

Maddie's mom stopped and looked at Maddie. "I will be just fine, Mads," she said, using her dad's pet name for his daughter. "Now before I go, this is for you."

She reached into her purse and handed her a folded-up note. "It's from Dad," she said, and Maddie started to get choked up. "I was going to hide it for you, but, well, I wasn't sure where he hid them. He didn't tell me that part, and then I worried that you might not find it at all, so . . ."

Maddie stared at the note and then looked up at her mom quizzically. Dad had died months ago. So where had the note come from?

"Dad and I talked about what your plans would be this summer," Mrs. Jacobs explained. "He wanted . . ."

She had to stop and take a breath. "No matter what happened, Dad wanted you to go to camp this year," she went on. "He knew how much you loved it and he wanted you to see your friends and have a ball like you always do. So he wrote you a note, just like he always did."

Maddie felt the tears flow now; she couldn't stop them.

"Oh, Maddie, no!" her mom said, hugging her. "This is a happy thing. Dad would want you to be happy, and I do too. Do you want to put the note away for a while or should we read it together?"

Maddie gulped. Part of her wanted to share the note with her mom, to talk and cry some more. Another part of her wanted to keep the letter between just her and her dad.

"I'm okay, Mom," she replied, slipping the note into the pocket of her shorts. "I usually read them before I go to bed."

Her mom looked worried, but she nodded. "Then that's what you should do," she said. She cupped Maddie's face in her hands and smiled at her. "Now it's time I left you with your friends. Give me a hug and promise me you'll have fun, okay?"

Maddie managed a smile and gave her mom a big bear

hug, and her mom gave her a kiss on the top of her head.

"I'll miss you, Madeline, but I want you to have a great summer, okay?"

Maddie nodded, and her mom kissed her one more time before getting into the car. Maddie waved as her mom drove away—down the road that led to the boys' camp instead of the road that led her out. She tried to signal her mom to stop, but Mrs. Jacobs didn't notice.

Oh well, Maddie thought. *She'll figure it out. We both will.*

THE GIRLS WERE FINISHING UNPACKING AND
catching up when Tara came into the cabin, a ball of happy energy.

"Hello, Hannahs!" she said, calling the girls by the name of their bunk. "Lunch is in ten minutes, but before we go I want to go over some bunk rules. Rule number one—"

"Have fun!" Liza yelled out, and then burst into a fit of giggles.

Tara grinned. "I was just about to say that. But seriously, we do have some rules around here. Number one, which I'm sure you all know, is no cell phones or electronic devices while you're at camp."

"What?" Amelia wailed. "You have got to be kidding!"

"That rule is clearly spelled out in the camp brochure," Tara said, looking Amelia squarely in the eye. "But if you brought any devices with you, we can keep them in the safe in the main office for you."

"What? No," Amelia said quickly.

"Good," Tara said, and then looked down at the clip-board she was carrying. "Everyone cleans up their own mess in the bunk, and we all help clean up the mess hall after meals. Lights out means lights out—no messing around. And if you have a problem with another camper, bring it to a counselor. We're here to help."

Libby raised her hand. "What about possums? Did you guys check for possums this year?"

Tara got a look of recognition on her face. "Oh, so you're the possum girl. Um, I'm not sure about that. I'll get back to you."

Amelia looked worried. "What about possums?"

"Don't worry, Libby will tell you all about it at lunch," Maddie promised her.

They headed to the mess hall, the largest building in the whole camp—a long, one-story rectangle covered with weathered wood shingles. Inside, campers were taking their seats at the round wood tables. A metal counter stretched along one side of the building, and Maddie smiled and waved at Mrs. Hancock, the camp cook. The plump, curly-haired woman smiled and waved back. "Hi, Maddie!" she called.

The six Hannahs sat down at one of the tables, and Amelia started to look around at the other campers.

"So, we have to all sit together when we eat?" she asked.

"Bunks always sit together," Maddie explained.

Liza nodded across the room, where the boys were starting to file in. "Yeah, and they separate the girls and boys across the room. No fun."

Maddie slyly glanced over to the boys' side, hoping to see the cute British boy. He was easy to spot because he was so tall, and she saw him laughing at something Jared was saying. Maddie quickly looked away. For a second she thought about pointing him out to her friends, but she felt a little silly.

Maybe later I'll tell Liza, she thought, grateful that their beds were right next to each other. Even though the rule was no talking after lights out, Maddie and Liza had held some of their most memorable conversations at night, whispered in the darkness.

Tara appeared at their table with a cheerful smile. "Okay, girls, time to line up for lunch!"

The girls joined the other campers on line to get lunch. Steam trays held hamburgers, veggie burgers, and fries. Next to the hot line was a salad bar loaded with lettuce and all kinds of vegetables. Next to that was the drink station. Samantha put a cup under the nozzle of one of the big jugs that were lined up, pulled the lever back, and watched a stream of neon orange liquid flow out.

She made a face. "What is this?"

"Bug juice," Maddie explained. "At least, that's what campers call it. It comes in three different flavors: sweet, sweeter, and sweetest. But you're probably better off with water."

Samantha cautiously took a sip. "I don't know. It's not so bad."

Amelia grimaced. "It looks disgusting."

The girls got drinks and then headed back to their table.

"Veggie burger number one," Emily announced, setting down her tray.

"What do you mean?" Samantha asked.

"It's the most popular vegetarian option at camp," Emily explained. "That and spaghetti. Last year I think I ate fifty veggie burgers, so this year I want to keep count."

"Why don't you just eat salad?" Libby asked, holding up a forkful of lettuce. "I love salad."

"Salad is okay, but it doesn't fill me up," Emily said with a sigh. "Plus, it gets boring."

"Everything here looks boring," Amelia complained.

"I know it might look that way now, but it's really fun," Maddie assured her. "After we eat, they'll show us the activity schedule. You'll see."

"Well," said Libby, peering around. "Has anyone checked out the boys yet?"

The girls all started craning their necks to see the boys at the other tables.

"Don't be so obvious!" hissed Libby, starting to giggle.

All the girls turned back around.

"Well some of them have grown a lot," said Emily.

"Some of them are kind of cute," said Samantha.

Amelia suddenly seemed very interested. "Which ones are our age?" she said.

Libby rolled her eyes. "The ones at the table behind us."

"Oh," said Amelia, sighing. "Them."

"The tall one is cute," said Samantha.

"Which is the tall one?" asked Emily.

"Um . . . the really tall one," said Samantha.

Maddie's ears perked up. Did she mean the British boy?

Just then Patty and Jim Lewis, the camp directors, were

standing up and wildly trying to get everyone's attention. "Campers!" called Jim. "It's time for announcements!"

"Welcome, campers, to Camp Wimoway!" said Patty, a short, athletic-looking woman with a neat haircut. "This is going to be a great season!"

Maddie joined in as the campers clapped and cheered. Liza put two fingers between her lips and let out a long, loud whistle.

"Now let's meet this year's fantastic counselors!" announced Jim, a trim man with a crew cut and glasses.

The counselors, young men and women in their twenties, like Tara, lined up next to the camp directors. Jim and Patty called out names and the campers cheered for each one.

Amelia leaned over to Maddie. "So what's with these two?" she asked, nodding her head toward Patty and Jim.

"Patty's family started the camp back in the fifties or something," Maddie explained. "Jim's her husband. They run the camp together."

Amelia rolled her eyes, like somehow that was a dumb job to have.

"They met at camp," said Maddie, watching Amelia.

Amelia stopped twirling her hair. "Really?" she said. She turned back around to take another look at the boys behind them. Maddie wondered if she was thinking she would marry one of them. Just as long as it wasn't her British boy.

Maddie didn't want to make her mind up about Amelia just yet—new campers always needed time to adjust—but something told her that Amelia might be trouble.

After the counselors were introduced, they handed out camp schedules. Maddie had been coming to camp so long that she knew the basic schedule by heart. Every year, though, the Lewises added some new activity choices to keep things interesting.

Camp Wimoway Schedule

7:30: wake-up

8:00: flag

8:15: breakfast

9:00: clean-up time

9:30: all-camp activity

10:30: activity 1

11:30: activity 2

12:30: lunch

1:15: siesta time

2:15: activity 3

3:15: instructional swimming

4:15: free time/snack time

5:15: activity 4

6:30: supper

7:30: evening program

8:30: downtime

9:00: curfew

9:30 lights out

"Seven thirty wake-up? Are they serious?" Amelia asked, her eyes wide.

"You get used to it," Maddie told her, but Amelia didn't look convinced.

Shy Samantha spoke up. "I don't get some of these things. What is siesta time?"

"They let us chill after lunch," Liza explained. "And that's when the little kids take a nap."

Maddie walked over to her and pointed to the schedule. "Flag is when we raise the camp flag outside the main office and get morning announcements. All-camp activity is something the whole camp does together, like a hike."

"You mean the boys and girls are together then?" Samantha asked.

Maddie nodded. "Right, and also during meals and flag and the evening program and free time," she explained. "The evening program is like a camp sing-along or something, and at free time and downtime you can do whatever you want."

"Thanks," Samantha said with a grateful smile.

"See? I told you guys there was instructional swim every day," Libby said with a groan. "I hate getting my hair wet!"

"Me too," Amelia agreed.

"Campers, today's schedule is a little different," Patty announced. "After lunch you'll have free time to choose your activities. Then at three o'clock we'll all meet at the new pool for swim tests, so we can place you in the proper instructional swim class."

"Fun," Libby said with another groan.

"It looks like there's other fun stuff in the schedule," Maddie pointed out.

"Let's go back to the cabin after this and pick what we want to do, so we can all do it together," Liza suggested.

A short while later the girls sat cross-legged on the

colorful rag rug on the cabin floor. Amelia flopped down on her bed, keeping her distance.

"Activity one: tennis or volleyball," Maddie read out loud.

"Tennis!" shouted Libby.

"Volleyball!" shouted Liza at the same time.

Emily sighed. "No crafts? I wish I could do crafts all day."

"I'll do whatever you guys do," Samantha said.

Emily shrugged. "I guess I will too, then, since I don't care."

Liza and Libby looked expectantly at Maddie. Normally she would have done whatever Liza wanted, but she had been hoping to take tennis this summer. Her mom had loved to play with her dad, and Maddie hoped to get good enough to play with her.

"I think tennis," Maddie said cautiously. "I'm trying to learn so I can play with my mom, but I'm really terrible at it."

Liza looked a little disappointed, but she seemed to understand.

"Ooh, it will be fun!" Libby promised. "I can help you, Maddie."

"Thanks," Maddie replied warmly.

"I guess tennis works," said Amelia. The girls turned

around and looked at her; they had completely forgotten about her sitting on the bed behind them.

Then they worked out the rest of the activity periods: drama, archery, and arts and crafts.

"Amelia, what are you doing?" Maddie asked as Amelia wandered over to the window.

"Plotting my escape out of here," Amelia replied darkly.

Then Tara came in. "All right, girls, time to slather on the sunscreen and suit up."

Thirty minutes later they were gathered around the pool with the rest of the campers. The afternoon sun was warm, and Maddie was itching to dive into the water. She loved any sports that took place in the water—kayaking, rowing, and especially swimming. So did Liza, which is one of the reasons they became friends in the first place.

The swim test was pretty simple. Four lanes had been set up across the pool, marked off by blue ropes held afloat by bright orange buoys. A counselor monitored each lane, and one by one the campers who knew how to swim were asked to jump or dive in the water, swim with a freestyle stroke to the other side of the pool, and swim back.

"Okay, Hannahs, you're up!" Tara told them.

Confident, Liza got to the front of the line. "Let's do this!" she said.

Tara blew a whistle, and Liza dove into the pool. As soon as she hit the water, she started to flounder, splashing her arms.

"It's s-s-so cold!" she complained.

"Come on, Liza, swim!" Maddie cheered.

Liza recovered and flawlessly swam across the pool and back. Then it was Maddie's turn. She braced herself now that she knew the water was cold. When she dove in, she told herself to just keep going, and then she swam to the other side and swiftly returned.

"Nice job!" Tara complimented her.

After Maddie's swim test, Samantha and Libby doggy-paddled their way across the pool. Amelia had a pretty good freestyle, but she got tired halfway back and finished with a lazy backstroke. Then, like Maddie, Emily had a nice strong swim.

"Good job, Hannahs," Tara said when they were done. "Samantha and Libby, you're in beginners. Amelia and Liza, you're in intermediate. Maddie and Emily are in advanced."

"Intermediate?" Liza asked, incredulous. "That is so not fair! I just got shocked by the cold water, that's all. Ask the swim counselor from last year, she'll tell you that I know what I'm doing."

"I have to base my placement on this test," Tara said evenly. "If you show improvement in the intermediate class, you can move up next week."

Liza frowned and looked away, and Maddie felt bad. That meant she and Liza wouldn't be in class together. That was another disappointment for her friend, Maddie knew—first the volleyball, now this, and then there was the fact that Liza wasn't staying the whole summer.

"Sorry, Liza," Maddie said, but her friend didn't say anything in response.

That night before lights out, Liza, Libby, and Emily sat cross-legged on Maddie's bed. Samantha was quietly reading a book, and Amelia had her head under the covers. The friends could see a soft glow shining through the blanket.

"I bet she's texting," Liza whispered, and Maddie put a finger to her lips.

"Shh," she said. "I think she's having a hard time adjusting."

"I am having a hard time adjusting to instructional

swim," Libby complained, and everyone laughed just as Tara walked in.

"Lights out, campers," she said, and then she noticed the four girls huddled together. "I see I've got the Four Musketeers in this cabin."

Everyone laughed but Liza.

"It won't be for long," she said sullenly. "I'll be leaving in the middle of the summer."

"But you'll be our fourth musketeer in spirit," Maddie promised.

"Yeah," Liza said, but she didn't sound convinced. She went over to her bed and pulled the covers over her.

"See you bright and early, Hannahs," Tara said when all the girls were settled, and then she turned out the light.

Maddie glanced over at Liza, eager to catch up, but Liza had already turned over to go to sleep. It looked like the night of whispering would have to wait. She drifted off to sleep, hoping that her friend was okay.

chapter 4

"MAIL CALL!" TARA ANNOUNCED, BURSTING INTO
the girls' bunk.

Amelia groaned. "Come on. I'm trying to siesta!" she
complained, pulling a pillow over her head.

It was the fourth day of camp, and Amelia hadn't
been adjusting to the early wake-up too well. Every day
after lunch she headed right for the cabin and crashed.
Today Libby was out getting some extra tennis practice,
Samantha was reading, Emily was knitting a canteen
cozy, and Liza and Maddie were playing a board game.

"Sorry, Amelia," Tara said, but she didn't lower
the naturally loud volume of her voice. "Maddie, there
are three letters for you."

"Three?" Maddie asked, looking up from the game
board. She didn't usually get a lot of mail at camp.

"I guess everyone's looking out for you," Tara said,

and Maddie suddenly felt uncomfortable.

Here we go, she thought.

"Maddie, how are you doing? Okay?" Tara asked in that concerned voice that Maddie had heard so much over the past year.

"Fine," Maddie said quickly. "Thanks for the letters."

"Looks like there's a package, too," Tara said with a grin. She handed over the mail and then left the cabin.

"What'd you get? What'd you get?" Liza asked, excited.

"Let me see," Maddie said. "Looks like a letter from Uncle Jay and Aunt Marie. And one from Aunt Ellen. And the package is from Grandma and Grandpa."

"Open it!" Liza urged.

Maddie obeyed. "Strawberry licorice, yay!" she said. She looked around the bunk. They weren't supposed to get any candy but most counselors didn't say anything about it. Maddie handed out pieces to everyone and stashed the package under her bed.

Amelia took the pillow off her head, suddenly interested. "Wow, that's a lot of mail."

"Yeah," Maddie said, but she didn't say much else. She knew her mom must have asked every relative to send her tons of mail to make her feel loved and all that stuff. But she didn't feel like explaining it to Amelia, or even talking about it with Liza.

"Yum, thanks!" Amelia said pleasantly as she bit into the licorice.

Libby walked in, dressed in a white shirt and shorts and carrying her tennis racket.

"Almost time for tennis," she said.

"Aren't you sick of tennis yet?" Liza asked.

"I will never be sick of tennis," Libby promised.

Emily put down her knitting needles. "Rats! I was almost finished," she said. "When I get older I'm going to run a summer camp for kids who just want to do crafts all day."

"That's actually a pretty good idea," Samantha said, looking up from her book.

"Thanks," Emily said. "Seth said he'll run it with me."

"Seth?" Maddie asked.

"You know, my height, glasses," Emily said. "He's in the Charles bunk, with that tall kid from England or whatever."

Maddie almost shouted, *I know him! He's totally the cutest boy ever!* but she stopped herself. She'd been keeping a lookout for BB (British Boy, her secret name for him), but she hadn't mentioned anything to Liza or any of her friends about him yet. Every time the girls started talking about boys they got distracted. They started talking about which girls' hair was longer or shorter and which counselors were the nicest (Tara was nice but strict; Wendy, who led the archery class, was strict but not supernice.) When they started talking about boys, even if they got distracted, they always ended up talking about boys again. It was hard to miss them this summer. It seemed like they were everywhere.

But today they dropped the "boys" conversation and just got ready to go to tennis.

And that felt pretty good to Maddie. Despite Tara constantly asking her if she was okay, and a lot more boy stuff this summer, she felt pretty normal so far. At school, all of her friends had been acting a little weird, but at camp it was like she was the same old Maddie.

Then something changed a few days later, when the second week of camp began. Maddie woke up to a humming sound, and as the fog of sleep lifted, she realized that someone was blow-drying their hair.

Maddie yawned and stretched. "What's going on?"

she asked Liza, who was standing in the middle of the cabin, impatiently tapping her foot.

"It's Amelia," Liza said. "She actually took a shower this morning."

"Really?" Maddie asked. Most campers took showers at night to wash off the day's dirt, and then jumped out of bed in the morning five minutes before flag. It was just how they did things. It didn't make sense to shower in the morning and then go do a sweaty activity an hour later.

"And she's been hogging one of the sinks in there," Liza said. There were only two sinks, which was a problem. "Emily is brushing her teeth now, and I can't do anything until Amelia gets out of there."

"I'm sure she won't be much longer," Maddie said. She got dressed in shorts and a T-shirt, but when she was finished she could still hear the blow-dryer going. Peeking into the sink area, she saw Liza furiously brushing her teeth and casting evil looks at Amelia.

Finally, Amelia stopped doing her hair—and picked up a makeup brush.

"Amelia, we're going to be late for flag," Liza said. "Why are you bothering, anyway?"

Amelia put down the brush. "In case you haven't

noticed, we have breakfast with the boys' camp," she said. "You can look like a mess if you want to, but not me." Then she went back to applying her makeup.

Liza's eyes narrowed. "Oh yeah? Well, how about if you don't back off of that mirror, I'll tell Tara about your nightly texting sessions."

Amelia scowled. "You wouldn't!"

"Try me," Liza said.

With a huff, Amelia gathered up her makeup and hair accessories and left the sink.

"Come on, Mads, you're up," Liza said.

Maddie hurried to the sink and brushed her teeth. As she was washing her face, she heard Tara's voice in the main room.

"You girls are late for flag! Let's go!"

Maddie took a look at herself. She smoothed down her hair and tried to pinch her cheeks so they looked rosy. She didn't look bad but, well, she looked like she just rolled out of bed.

Maddie scrambled to finish up and followed the rest of the Hannahs out of the bunk. When they got to flag, she suddenly felt self-conscious—several girls from the other bunks had followed Amelia's lead, doing their hair and putting on lip gloss and blush. Maddie scoped out the crowd and spotted BB talking with some of the boys. If the girls impressed them, they didn't seem to notice.

Emily nudged her and pointed to some of the made-up girls. "They look ridiculous, right? This is camp!"

"Yeah," Maddie whispered back. But even though she was relieved that the boys didn't seem to care, she wondered if maybe Amelia had a point. Not about the lip gloss, maybe, but it couldn't hurt to look nice in the morning, could it?

By dinnertime that night, everyone was equally hot and disheveled from the day's activities. The girls got on the food line and piled their plates with chicken fingers, mashed potatoes, and green beans.

"Veggie burger number four," Emily announced, holding it up for everyone to see.

Liza picked up the salt shaker and eyed her mashed potatoes. "If I were vegetarian I'd eat mashed potatoes every day. Yum!" she said, then tipped over the shaker to salt the potatoes . . . and the loose cap fell off, dumping a mound of salt onto her food.

"No!" Liza wailed. At the tables around her, other

girls were shrieking and laughing in surprise as the same thing happened to them.

"What's going on?" Samantha asked.

"It's the oldest camp prank in the book," Maddie replied. "The boys loosened the caps of all the salt and pepper shakers on the girls' tables. You can't tell, so when you go to shake it, the caps fall off."

She nodded to the boys' side of the mess hall, where the boys were all cracking up at the girls' reactions—even BB.

Samantha started to giggle. "Sorry, Liza, but it's kind of funny."

"Maybe," Liza said, her eyes narrowing. "But if they're out of mashed potatoes up there I'm going to swipe them from the first boy's plate I see."

She got up and stomped back to the food line.

"Wow, she seems mad," Amelia remarked.

"Don't worry, she'll be fine," Maddie said. "I pity those boys when Liza gets her revenge!"

"BIG BUFFALO COMES FROM THE MOUNTAIN FAR, *far away!*

Far, far away, woop, woop, woop.

Far, far away, woop, woop, woop!"

Maddie sang along with the other campers, ending with a big, loud WOOP and then bursting into giggles.

"Great job, campers!" Patty Lewis cheered. "Enjoy the rest of your night!"

Maddie and Liza stood up and stretched. They'd been sitting cross-legged on a blanket during the camp sing-along. Maddie looked up at the shining stars scattered across the black sky overhead. Her dad had loved to show her the constellations.

See that there? That's the Big Dipper, he would say. *And see how that star over there looks like it's twinkling? Those are special stars. You can wish on them. Make a wish, Mads. Go ahead.*

When she was little, Maddie wished for things like chocolate ice cream or a new stuffed animal. As she spotted a twinkling star in the sky above her now, the power of wishing suddenly felt like a big responsibility. What would she wish for now? That Dad had never gotten sick? That Mom would be happy again? Or was it okay to wish for something frivolous, like wishing there'd be s'mores at the campfire tomorrow night? It didn't really matter, anyway, because wishes weren't real. If they were, Dad would still be alive.

"Earth to Mads," Liza said, interrupting her thoughts. "You okay?"

"What?" Maddie asked. "Oh, yeah, sure. Let's go get some cookies and milk."

They rolled up their blanket and headed over to the mess hall, following the rest of the campers. After the evening program there was a half hour of downtime before curfew, and most campers went to the mess hall for cookies and milk. Maddie and Liza found Libby, Emily, and Samantha sitting on some benches in the quad in front of the mess hall with three girls from the Betty bunk: Holly, Ava, and Morgan. They were all whispering and giggling.

"What's going on?" Liza asked as she and Maddie took a seat next to Libby.

"We're voting on who the cutest boy is at camp," Libby replied. "So far, Brandon has the most votes."

"Totally," Liza said, nodding. "He's like, way cuter this year for some reason."

Maddie shrugged. "I think he looks the same," she said. "Maybe a little taller."

"I think that British kid is pretty cute," said Morgan, a girl with big brown eyes and curly blond hair.

"That's Gabriel," Emily said. "Seth says he's pretty nice."

Gabriel. Maddie's heart skipped a beat. Wasn't that the name of an angel? It figured he would have such a beautiful name. She scanned the quad and spotted Gabriel still over by the fire. Something about the way the firelight danced across his face made her heart jump again.

Is this what it's like to have a crush on someone? she wondered.

"What about you, Maddie?" Libby asked.

Maddie snapped out of her thoughts. "Um, I don't know," she replied, although it wasn't true. She definitely thought Gabriel was the cutest, but the thought of saying it out loud still felt weird.

"Well, I vote for Brandon," Liza said, and Maddie noticed something in her friend's voice she hadn't before. Was Liza crushing on Brandon?

"Brandon's good at tennis, so I'll vote for him too," Libby said.

"Shh! He's coming!" Ava hissed, and the girls quieted down as Brandon walked by with some other boys. When they had passed, the girls collapsed into giggles again.

She snuck another look over at Gabriel, beautiful Gabriel. Liza was crazy, he was way cuter than Brandon. Not even close.

The next morning the rushing water sound of the shower woke Maddie. She glanced at the clock on her dresser and saw that it was only 6:35. It had to be Amelia, up early to do her hair again, Maddie guessed, but then she saw that Amelia was still asleep. Liza's bed, though, was empty.

Maddie sat up in bed and yawned. Once she was awake, it was tough to go back to sleep. A few minutes later Liza emerged from the bathroom, fully dressed and rubbing her hair with a towel.

"What are you doing?" Maddie whispered.

Liza glanced at Amelia. "I hate to say it, but I think

she's right," she said. "I mean, it can't hurt to look nice at breakfast, right?"

"I guess not," Maddie said thoughtfully. After all, half of the girls at camp had taken Amelia's lead and were getting dressed up for breakfast. She didn't want to stand out. She thought of Gabriel looking over at her with her hair matted down from sleep and the pillow marks still on her face. She shuddered. That would be bad.

Maddie scrambled out of bed and got ready for a shower. When she got out, Libby was in the other shower and Samantha was waiting to take one. Amelia was standing behind Samantha, looking annoyed.

"You guys could have told me you were getting up early too," she complained.

Maddie got dressed and then dried her hair, using the attachment that made it nice and straight. When she finished, she had to admit that she looked nicer than she had since she came to camp. Maybe Gabriel would notice.

Then Tara poked her head into the bathroom. "Come on, girls! We're going to be late! Who cares if your hair isn't straight? This is *camp*!"

"Coming!" Maddie said quickly. She ran into the cabin's main room, where Emily was sitting at her dresser, gluing plastic gems onto a picture frame made of craft sticks. Her curly hair was just as messy as ever.

"You too, Emily," Tara said.

"No problem," Emily said, standing. "I've been ready since I woke up."

The girls rushed to make flag, mostly polished, although Amelia's hair was still wet at the ends. Maddie didn't pay attention to any of the morning announcements; she was too busy casting glances at Gabriel. Gabriel. She would never get tired of that name.

At breakfast Maddie picked up the pepper shaker to use on her scrambled eggs, when Liza put a hand over hers, stopping her.

"Better check first," Liza warned, and Maddie obeyed. The cap was tight.

"Thanks," she said. "So, what are you planning to do to get back at them? Is anyone planning anything?"

"I'm working on it," Liza said. "It's got to be perfect."

After they ate, the girls went back to the cabin to clean up and change into swimsuits for the all-camp activity. It was lake sports this week, Maddie's favorite. Campers could choose between going out in a rowboat, canoe, or kayak.

Maddie shoved some clothes into a drawer and quickly

changed, putting her hair up into a ponytail.

"What's the rush, Mads?" Liza asked.

"I want to get a kayak today," she said. "Those are the most fun."

Liza nodded. "Yeah, they're the fastest."

Maddie waved and raced out the cabin door. "See you there!" she called behind her.

She jogged down the wooded path to Lake Wimoway, a lake about the size of a football field, which was a pretty good size for a summer camp, or so Maddie's dad had always said. The boats were lined up along the sandy beach, and an old wooden dock bobbed on the water off shore. The water out by the dock was deep enough for diving and swimming.

Maddie was one of the first campers to the lake, so after nodding to Shannon, the counselor in charge of lake sports, who smiled and waved to her, she grabbed a life preserver and headed toward a blue kayak. She dragged it into the water and hopped in, then gripped the double-ended paddle in both hands and headed out.

She glided quickly across the water, rhythmically dipping the paddle left, then right, then left. . . . Then she heard a voice behind her.

"Hey, mate, wait for me!"

She turned with a smile, recognizing the accent. Gabriel was paddling beside her! Her heart started dancing around again.

"Hi," Maddie said shyly.

"That was right brilliant to get here early and grab a kayak," Gabriel said. "They're the best, aren't they?"

"Definitely," Maddie agreed with a smile. "So I guess that makes you right brilliant too."

Gabriel smiled back. "You're fast," he told her. "Not like some of those blokes in my cabin. They splash around like ducks in the water."

Maddie laughed. "I know, it's like their paddles are dangerous weapons or something," she joked. "But they usually get better by the end of the week. The counselors are pretty good at teaching stuff."

They paddled together in silence for a little while, making their way all around the lake. Inside her head, Maddie couldn't help singing, *Row, row, row your boat . . .* Her dad had always sung that—loudly—whenever they went kayaking or canoeing. She was very aware of Gabriel paddling next to her and she didn't quite know what to say or do, so she was grateful for the rhythm of the boat and the slap, slap, slap of the paddle on the water. Soon Maddie was deep in a groove, paddling and singing the song in her head.

Then, to her embarrassment, she realized that she had started to sing out loud! She was about to stop when she heard Gabriel join her.

"Merrily, merrily, merrily, merrily. Life is but a dream!"

They sang together, playfully splashing at each other, until they heard Shannon's whistle across the lake calling them in.

"Race you!" Gabriel called out, and Maddie didn't hesitate, paddling like crazy and laughing just as hard. She beat him to the shore by a foot.

"Good race!" Gabriel congratulated her.

"Thanks!" Maddie replied, and then suddenly became self-conscious. There is no graceful way to get out of a kayak; Maddie usually just tipped the boat on its side and spilled out into the water, but she decided that wasn't the best thing to do in front of Gabriel. She set aside the paddle, and gripping the sides of the boat, she started to stand up. The kayak rocked unsteadily back and forth.

Splash! It tipped over, sending Maddie into the lake.

"Hang on!" Gabriel cried. He jumped out of his kayak, tipping his boat over too. Maddie laughed and splashed him, and Gabriel splashed her back.

Shannon blew her whistle again, and Maddie finally got on her feet and dragged the kayak back to the sand. Liza was waiting for her with a knowing smile on her face.

"He's cuuuuute!" Liza said.

Maddie just shrugged. "Oh, him?" But inside, her heart was smiling.

MADDIE COULDN'T STOP THINKING ABOUT Gabriel. She thought about him during tennis, and her crazy serves kept going out of bounds. She thought about him during drama, when she was supposed to be pretending she was a piece of bacon frying in a pan, but she forgot to move.

"I need some more sizzle from you, Maddie!" the counselor yelled, and everyone laughed.

At lunchtime she absently stabbed at her salad with a fork and kept looking at the boys' side, hoping to catch a glimpse of him. Gabriel noticed and waved to her, and she smiled back. Then she quickly stopped herself. Had anyone noticed?

"Veggie burger number nine," Emily announced. No, things were back to normal.

After lunch, the girls headed back to the cabin for

siesta. It was a hot day, the kind of day where the air feels heavy, so the girls lazed on the porch steps, too sticky and tired to do anything but talk. Libby pulled out a notebook with a glittery pink cover and a purple pen.

"Okay, we're rating the Charles bunk now," she announced.

Charles bunk? That was Gabriel's bunk. "Rating what?" Maddie asked.

"Boys, of course," Libby replied.

Maddie was confused. "I thought you did that the other night."

"Weren't you listening at lunch?" Libby asked. "Last night we were talking generally. Then we got the idea to rate the boys in each cabin."

Maddie started to feel excited. Maybe now she could finally talk about Gabriel with her friends.

"Okay," Libby began thoughtfully. "Charles bunk is Evan, Scott, Gabriel, Kyle, Ryan, and Seth."

"Evan is definitely last," Liza said.

"Why is he last?" Samantha asked, puzzled. "He's got nice eyes."

"He's cute, but he never talks to girls, he only jokes around with the boys," Liza pointed out.

"Then Scott should be on the bottom too, because he's really quiet," Amelia said.

Libby nodded. "Good point," she said, jotting something in her notebook.

"You can be quiet and still be cute," Samantha said. "And nice."

"Maybe," Liza said. "But to be crush-worthy, you have to be friendly and talk to the girls."

"That's why Gabriel should be number one," Amelia said. "He talks to girls and he's super cute."

Maddie was stunned. "What?" she asked, a little too loudly, and Amelia cocked her head.

"Oh no, do you like him too?" Amelia asked innocently.

Maddie blushed. It hadn't occurred to her that someone else would have a crush on Gabriel. But of course they would! He was amazing.

"He's really awesome," Amelia pressed on. "You do like him, right, Maddie?"

Maddie couldn't speak. She didn't know what to say. It would be weird to admit that she liked Gabriel too, wouldn't it?

"Are you okay, Mads?" Liza asked.

"Yeah," Maddie muttered. "Just tired." Then she got up, walked into the cabin, and flopped down on her bed.

Maddie buried her head in her pillow. She didn't feel like crying, exactly; she just wanted to melt into the mattress and disappear, at least for a while.

She heard Amelia sigh. "All I said was that maybe she's not the only one to like him. Geez!" Then she heard Liza's voice float through the open window.

"You have to be careful around her," Liza scolded. "Her dad just died. Just take it easy on her, okay?"

A swell of frustration rose up in Maddie's chest. It was cool of Liza to stand up for her, but hearing it made her realize that the death of Maddie's dad had been on Liza's mind all along. She thought everything was back to normal here at camp, that everyone was treating her like they always had. But maybe she was wrong. Had she been in some kind of bubble, not noticing the whispers and stares?

Maddie wiped a tear from her eye. It had felt so good to feel normal again—but now it felt like nothing would ever be the same.

chapter 7

AFTER SIESTA, MADDIE LEFT THE CABIN WITH HER guard up, studying the campers and counselors to see if they were looking at her differently or whispering about her. But when she went to archery in the field near the boys' camp, she found that having to focus so hard on the activity took her mind off things. She listened to the counselor and breathed slowly and deeply each time she pulled back the bow, concentrating. The effort paid off, and she got three bull's-eyes, the most she'd ever got in one session.

At arts and crafts, she sat with Liza, Libby, Emily, and Samantha as a counselor named Kathy showed them how to make beaded necklaces. The room got quiet as the girls thoughtfully picked out which beads they wanted to use.

"Pink, pink, and pink," Libby said, plucking beads from the organizer tray.

Emily started to choose one of every color. "I want to do a rainbow one," she said.

Samantha held up a sparkly lavender bead. "Isn't this one pretty? Maybe I'll do all different shades of purple."

Maddie and Liza reached for the blue beads at the same time. They grinned at each other.

"They remind me of the water," Maddie said, and Liza nodded.

"Me too."

Stringing the beads was nice and peaceful, and Maddie soon felt calmer and more relaxed. When she was done, she put her finished creation around her neck, and Liza did the same.

"We're like twins," Maddie said with a grin.

"Right," Liza agreed. "Only with different color hair and different color eyes."

"Hey, twins don't have to look alike," Maddie pointed out, and they both laughed.

Maddie felt even better as the day went on. Emily ate her tenth veggie burger, and Liza started joking around about drama class. She held up a piece of meatloaf on her fork.

"I can't believe that Alyssa keeps making us pretend

that we're bacon frying in a pan," she said. "I bet she's going to make us act like meatloaf next."

"How do you act like meatloaf?" Maddie asked.

Liza slumped back in her chair and closed her eyes. "Maybe like this. You just . . . loaf."

Everyone started cracking up. Emily stood up perfectly straight with her arms at her sides. "I've got one!"

"What are you supposed to be?" Libby asked.

"An ear of corn!" Emily replied, and everyone cracked up again.

Maddie smiled to herself as the girls ate their dinner. It was nice just talking and hanging out and not having to worry about the boys or how they looked. It was kind of like how it used to be. Except, of course, that Maddie never really stopped thinking about Gabriel completely. She wondered if she gave him a bracelet she made, if he would wear it. There was a girl at school who gave one of the boys a friendship bracelet to wear and it was a pretty big deal. Maddie would never have the nerve, though. Would she? She picked at her food and thought about it.

At the evening program that night some of the counselors told a spooky story, and then Maddie and her friends headed to the mess hall to grab some milk and cookies and hang in the quad. Maddie was about to settle down on one of the benches, oatmeal cookie in hand, when she felt a tap on her shoulder.

She whirled around and saw Gabriel standing there.

"Hullo," he said. "You did a right good job of beating me this morning. How did you get to be such a good boater?"

It took Maddie a moment to realize that he was actually trying to have a conversation with her, and she got a little flustered.

"Well, yeah, I guess, I've been, um, doing it a long time," she replied.

Gabriel sat down on one of the large rocks in the quad, and it felt natural to Maddie to sit down next to him. She spotted her friends on the bench, pointing at them and giggling, and Maddie blushed a little, but she stayed put.

"Actually, my dad is the one who taught me how to kayak," Maddie said. "He was really very good at it. Canoeing, too."

"You're lucky," Gabriel said. "My mum and dad hate the water. I learned how to row at school."

"Wow, that's cool," Maddie said. "We don't do anything like that at our school. Just basketball and soccer and stuff."

Gabriel shook his head. "I still can't get used to the whole 'soccer' thing," he said. "It's always been 'football' to me."

Maddie wanted to ask him a lot. She figured he was from England, but then what was he doing here? And why did his mom sound American? But those questions felt kind of personal, so she steered the conversation back to boating.

"I remember I was pretty bad at first, but Dad showed me the right way to hold the paddles and how to keep my balance," she said.

Gabriel nodded. "Balance is definitely key."

They talked some more, but soon they heard the mess hall bell ring, the signal that meant downtime was over.

"Well, see you," Maddie said shyly.

"Right. See you," Gabriel said.

When she got to the bunk, all of the Hannahs were hanging out on the porch, waiting.

"Maddie!" Liza screamed. *"He likes you!"*

"Shhh!" Maddie said, but she was secretly pleased, and her friends didn't stop. The other girls joined in, chanting, "He likes you! He likes you!"

"And I knew you liked him," Amelia said, pointing at her.

"Well, I guess," Maddie said, and suddenly everything felt weird again. "I mean, we just talked, that's all."

"But he doesn't talk to other girls alone like that," Liza pointed out, and Amelia looked a little stung by the comment. "That means that he likes you."

"All that means is that he wanted to talk," Maddie said. "Like we're talking now."

Libby dramatically put a hand to her face. "Ah! Zee poor girl! She is so blind!" she said in a bad French accent.

"Libby's right," Emily said matter-of-factly. "He definitely likes you."

"Okay, okay, he likes me, whatever," Maddie said, hoping to end the conversation quickly. "Come on, we'd better go in before Tara gets here."

Liza shuddered, pretending to be afraid. "Beware the wrath of Tara!"

The girls trooped inside the cabin and got ready for bed. Maddie got under the covers and closed her eyes as the nighttime sounds of chirping crickets and croaking frogs filled the cabin. Normally these sounds lulled her to sleep, but she couldn't help thinking about what her friends had said.

Maybe Gabriel did like her. But what did that mean?

How was it different from the way she liked her other friends, or the way she liked someone like Brandon, even?

It's all so complicated, she thought, but the crickets and the frogs won out, and she finally drifted off to sleep.

chapter 8

DEAR MADDIE,

I hope you are having fun at camp. Things have been pretty quiet here except that the Taylors got a new dog, a Chihuahua, and it yips and yelps all day long.

Grandma and Grandpa told me that they've written you several letters. Did you get them? I know you are busy but they would love to hear back from you.

Curled up in her bed during siesta, Maddie read the rest of her mother's letter. The third week of camp had just started, and she hadn't written a single letter in reply to any of her relatives. Her mom was right—she'd been really busy. During siesta she always felt too sleepy to do anything useful, and she'd been using most of her free periods to practice tennis with Libby. Playing tennis twice a day wasn't her favorite thing in the world, but Libby said she was getting better, and she knew she would impress her mom by the time summer was over.

Maddie groaned loudly. "I wish we could just text everybody. It's so much faster!"

"I don't know," Emily said. "I kind of like writing letters. It's more personal."

Liza looked up from her bed. "Still haven't written those letters yet, Mads?"

Maddie shook her head. "No, and now Mom's getting on my case."

Liza sat up. "I have an idea. Remember a few years ago, we picked those flowers and squashed them, and then we glued them to cards? My mom went crazy over hers."

Maddie nodded. "Those came out nice. Maybe we could pick some flowers today during free time. I saw some growing along the edges of the soccer meadow."

"Tomorrow, okay?" Liza asked. "Emily said she'd help me finish up this birdhouse I'm making in arts and crafts. I'm trying to finish it before the end of the week."

"Sure," Maddie replied. "Tomorrow. That means I

can nap for ten whole minutes now and not worry about writing letters."

Then she leaned back on her bed, putting the pillow over her head, and a folded piece of paper slipped out of the pillowcase. Maddie touched it—it was the note from her father. She still hadn't opened it. Sometimes she took it out at night to see if it smelled like her dad, but it didn't. But she could see a smudge of blue ink on one side of the note, like it always was with Dad's letters. He was left-handed, so his hand always had blue or black ink smudged on it.

It's one of the curses of a creative mind, he would say, and Maddie smiled, remembering.

"Come on, Mads! Archery time!" Liza said, playfully shaking her, and Maddie quickly slipped the note back under the pillowcase. Maybe she'd read it soon, but not now.

The next day was another blur of camp activities. After instructional swim in the afternoon, Maddie went back to the cabin to change for free time.

"Maddie, we're hitting the courts, right?" Libby asked.

"Sure," Maddie replied. She and Libby had been practicing regularly, and they'd gotten into a routine. As she tied the laces of her sneakers, she had a nagging feeling that she might be forgetting something, but she brushed it off.

It was another bright, hot day, but thankfully the tennis courts were mostly shaded in the afternoon. Maddie and Libby always found an open court; not many campers used their free time to practice tennis. They either relaxed, hung out, or played impromptu games of football in the soccer meadow.

Libby jogged to one side of the court, and Maddie took her place at the other.

"Okay, I'll serve," Libby said. "You're doing a lot better, Maddie. Just remember what I said, and keep your eyes on the ball."

Maddie focused on Libby, determined to return the ball. Libby swung, and Maddie watched the ball come toward her. She followed it as it veered to the right, brought her racket back, and swung.

Smack! The ball hit the racket, and Maddie sent it soaring across the net . . . and out of bounds.

"Rats!" Maddie cried.

"It's okay," Libby told her. "You're making contact. But I think you turned your wrist a little when you swung, so the ball went wild. Let's try again."

Maddie nodded, trying not to get frustrated. Even after taking tennis lessons in the spring, she always seemed to have the same problems.

Libby served again, and Maddie kept her eye on the ball and focused on her grip at the same time. The ball soared over the net and over Maddie's head, and even though she ran back as fast as she could, she just couldn't get to it in time.

"Rats!" she cried again.

"That was a tough one," Libby said. "When you play you have to be able to get anywhere on the court really fast. My instructor told me to jump rope when I work out to build up speed and coordination."

"Do we have any jump ropes at camp?" Maddie asked.

"I'm not sure," Libby replied. "Anyway, what we're doing is good practice too."

Maddie sighed. "All right. Keep them coming."

Libby helped her practice for a half hour, and Maddie managed to hit quite a few balls over the net without them going out of bounds.

"You're really doing great," Libby assured her as they walked back to the bunk.

"Thanks," Maddie said. "It's really nice of you to help me."

As they approached the bunk, Maddie saw Liza sitting on top of the porch steps. She looked upset, and suddenly Maddie remembered—they were supposed to meet to get flowers today!

"Liza, I'm so sorry!" Maddie said, running ahead of Libby. "I totally forgot."

"Well I didn't," Liza said, a little crossly. But she softened when she saw Maddie's face. "It's okay. Don't worry about it."

"We can do it tomorrow," Maddie promised.

"Well, we'd better do it soon," Liza said. "I'm not going to be here much longer, you know."

That's when it hit Maddie—the third week of camp was almost over already, which meant that Liza would be going home in a few days.

"Tomorrow, I promise," Maddie said. "Come on, let's walk to arts and crafts."

"Okay," Liza said, and she didn't seem so mad anymore.

Maddie was relieved that Liza wasn't hurt. In a way, though, she didn't mind Liza getting mad at her. She was treating her like she normally would, instead of being fake nice.

Still, though, she wanted to make things up to Liza somehow. Ever since they'd come to camp, she knew Liza was jealous that Maddie was staying on with Libby and Emily. But Liza was her best camp friend—no, her best friend anywhere. So she definitely had to make it up to her, even though she didn't have much time left.

chapter 9

"I'D BETTER SEE SIX GIRLS READY FOR FLAG WHEN I walk in here," Tara called from outside the cabin door. "If not, I'm going to confiscate your blow-dryers!"

Maddie put down her hairbrush and rushed to the door along with the other girls. The only one who wasn't scrambling was Emily. She got up off her bed, stretched, and lined up behind Maddie.

Tara entered the cabin and smiled when she saw them all. "That's more like it," she said. "All right, then. Flag time!"

Every morning, campers hoisted the Camp Wimoway flag up a tall pole outside the camp directors' office. At night, the flag came down. This morning, as the girls made their way to the morning assembly, they saw groups of campers pointing up at the flag and giggling. Instead of the usual camp flag, a pair of pink, polka-dotted underwear was flapping in the breeze.

Samantha looked confused. "How did that get up there?"

"It's those boys," Liza replied. "Another classic prank. They swiped some girl's undies and ran them up the flag."

Libby gasped. "Oh my gosh, those are Emily's!"

The girls turned to look at their friend, who was smiling. "They look awesome, don't they?"

Maddie laughed. "Yes, they do."

Amelia rolled her eyes. "If those were mine, I'd never admit it. Those polka dots are hideous."

But Emily didn't care. "Everyone salute my underwear!" she yelled, raising her arms in the air, and the boys started cracking up.

Liza was frowning. "If I were you, I'd be mad," she said. "Not because you should be embarrassed about your underwear, but because it's an invasion of privacy. Those boys snuck into our cabin. That hits too close to home."

Maddie suddenly knew how to make things up to her best friend. She leaned over and whispered in Liza's ear.

"Let's get them back," Maddie said. "I'll help you. I have an idea."

Liza turned to her, and her blue eyes were sparkling. "I knew I could count on you, Mads."

For the rest of the day, Maddie and Liza were insepa-rable. They paired up during tennis, laughing hysterically as they both sent the ball flying in crazy directions. In acting, they practiced being a baked potato and a fried chicken leg. At instructional swim, Liza surprised Maddie by showing up for the advanced class.

"Tara said I was ready," Liza said, grinning. "Of course, I thought I was ready three weeks ago, but whatever."

During free time, they headed to the soccer meadow to pick flowers. Colorful wildflowers dotted the overgrown border of the meadow, and lacy green ferns grew in the woods on the meadow's north side.

"I think we were, like, eight the last time we did this," Maddie remarked. "It's hard to believe it was that long ago."

"I know, right?" Liza nodded. She leaned down to pluck a tiny blue flower nestled in the grass.

"So much has changed since then," Maddie said, and she regretted the words as soon as she said them. It was true, but the last thing she wanted to do was talk about her dad now, when she was so free and happy.

But Liza just smiled. "Yeah, things change, but we'll always be friends." *Which was the exact right thing to*

say, Maddie thought, *and just another reminder of why Liza was her best friend.*

"Always," Maddie replied.

Liza stood up. "Come on, it's time for arts and crafts. Let's see what we can do with these."

Carrying their treasures in paper lunch sacks, they trooped across the meadow, past the bunks, to the craft cabin. Maddie found herself swiveling her head around as they walked across camp. It was almost second nature at this point to be on the lookout for Gabriel. Which was silly. After all, would she march up to him? Go over and just talk to him? Probably not. But well . . . why not? She was lost in thought.

"Earth to Maddie!" said Liza. "What do you keep looking for? More flowers?"

Maddie looked down so Liza couldn't see her blush. She felt bad. She was supposed to be having quality time with Liza, not thinking about Gabriel. "Uh, yeah, just looking for some more flowers," she said.

Twice the size of one of the bunks, the arts and crafts cabin was stuffed with shelves containing paint, yarn, glue, glitter, beads, fake fur, and every other craft supply Maddie could ever imagine. When they arrived, Emily was already there, gluing plastic gems onto a wooden box she had painted bright purple. The rectangular box had high sides and was open on top with a handle, almost like a toolbox.

"What are you working on?" Maddie asked.

"It's a craft caddy, like a portable container for my basic craft supplies," Emily said. "I've been working on it all through free time. What do you think? Does it need more gems?"

"It looks pretty sparkly to me," Maddie replied. "It's beautiful."

Liza dumped the contents of her bag onto the table. "So, do you think you can help us make cards out of these? I forget how we did it last time."

Emily frowned, thinking. "Well, if you want to dry or press the flowers so they'll last a long time, that will take, like, a week."

"I don't have a week to do that," Liza said. "I'm leaving in a few days."

"Not a problem," Emily said. She started putting some of the fern leaves and smaller flowers aside. "I bet if you spray these with some acrylic spray, they'll last for a while. Long enough to mail them, anyway. You can spray them outside, and when the stuff dries just glue them to the front of the card."

"Cool," Maddie said. "Where's the spray?"

Emily pointed. "In that closet over there," she said, and then went back to gluing more gems onto her craft caddy.

Maddie and Liza went to the closet and looked for the spray. Maddie noticed a big jar of petroleum jelly on the shelf. She picked it up and grinned at Liza.

"Just what we need," she whispered.

Liza looked around to make sure no one was looking at them. Then she took the jar from Maddie and slipped it into the empty brown bag.

"Perfect," she said, nodding at Maddie. "Now let's go make some cards."

With Emily's help, the girls created a dozen cards decorated with beautiful flowers and leaves.

"Now I have to start writing those letters," Maddie said, holding up a card with a little white daisy on the front. "I'll definitely, definitely do it tomorrow."

"I'll remind you," Liza said. "Because after I'm gone, I want to make sure you write me a letter too."

"Of course I will," Maddie promised.

That night, the girls sang loudly at the campfire,

cracking up after each silly song. When the sing-along was over, they headed to the mess hall for milk and cookies. Maddie saw Gabriel waiting by their rock for her. He looked at Maddie expectantly as she approached.

Maddie looked at Liza.

"It's okay," Liza said, her eyes twinkling. "See you back at the bunk."

"Hey," Maddie said, walking to the rock.

Gabriel slid over, offering her a seat. "I got you a cookie," he said, "and some chocolate milk."

"Thanks," Maddie said, taking the snack from him. She noticed she didn't feel as flustered as she usually did. Things just felt . . . normal.

Is that good or bad? she asked herself, starting to worry. Didn't the sweaty palms, heart-pumping thing mean she had a crush? So was her crush gone?

"You and your friend are good singers," Gabriel said, and Maddie blushed a little.

"Yeah, we were kind of loud tonight," she said, and then her worried thoughts flew away. "So, where are you from, exactly?"

Gabriel smiled. "London," he replied. "I thought it was fairly obvious."

"But your mom," Maddie said, and then she stopped herself. Gabriel had seemed pretty embarrassed by his mom that first day. Maybe she shouldn't bring it up?

But Gabriel just laughed. "She's American. My dad is British, but they got divorced last year, so mum and I came to America to live."

"Wow," Maddie said. "That's a big change."

Gabriel nodded. "Getting used to another country is pretty big. I miss my friends, but I miss my dad the most. He's pretty far away."

So is mine, Maddie thought, and even though it wasn't exactly the same, she knew how Gabriel must feel.

"Have you started school yet?" Maddie asked, changing the subject.

"No, we just moved in June," Gabriel replied, and he suddenly looked nervous. "I start in the fall. My mum thought it would be a good idea for me to go off and have a nice summer at camp while she gets everything settled at home. If you ask me, she wanted to park me somewhere while she got things sorted out. I'd rather be settling in at home."

A dark looked crossed his face, and then softened. "No offense or anything!"

Maddie shook her head. "It's okay. I think my mom dumped me here for the whole summer too!"

Gabriel didn't ask why, and Maddie didn't tell him. Soon it was time for curfew. She said good-bye to Gabriel and gave him a big smile, then she headed toward the cabin with a warm, glowy feeling in her chest. Maddie found herself whispering with Liza after lights out, just like they used to.

"So you really like Gabriel?" Liza asked.

"I think so," Maddie whispered. "But it's confusing. I'm not sure how I'm supposed to feel."

"I know what you mean," Liza replied. "I thought I liked Brandon, but now I don't know. It's like you're sup-posed to like somebody, but why? What would make me like Brandon? I mean, sure he's cute and he's nice, but so are a lot of boys. And sometimes he can be a little bit of a jerk. I'm pretty sure he's the one who stole Emily's underwear."

"Well, Gabriel's nice," Maddie said. "I don't think he would ever steal anyone's underwear."

"That's cool," Liza replied. "So if he's nice, then just keep hanging out with him. Why not?"

"Why not?" Maddie agreed.

"Will you two be quiet?" Amelia hissed.

"Stop texting!" Liza hissed back, and Amelia didn't say another word.

Liza grinned at Maddie. "Night, Mads."

"Night," Maddie replied, and then she feel into a deep and lovely sleep.

chapter 10

THE NEXT NIGHT MADDIE AND LIZA QUICKLY changed before dinner. Maddie put on black shorts and a black tank top, and Liza wore purple shorts with a navy blue T-shirt.

"Do you have it?" Maddie asked as they got ready to leave the bunk.

Liza grinned and held up a small drawstring bag. "We're good to go."

They nervously ate dinner, hoping that no one would notice their unusual change of clothes. But everything was normal.

"Veggie burger twenty-one," Emily announced as the girls brought their trays to the table.

"Oh my gosh, Emily, you are going to turn into a veggie burger before camp is over!" Maddie exclaimed.

"I know," Emily said glumly. "But I've got a plan. I'm

making a new apron for Mrs. Hancock, and then I'll suggest that she get some tofu into this place."

"I hope she likes glitter," Amelia said.

Liza made a face. "Tofu? I'm so glad I'm leaving in two days."

"Hey, I like tofu too," Libby said, standing up for Emily.

"I like it in miso soup," Samantha said quietly.

"Well, then it's a good thing you're all staying," Liza said, and Maddie glanced at her, worried. But Liza didn't look upset, and Maddie felt relieved.

After dinner they all filed out for the evening program. Because the first camp session was ending soon, the counselors had put together a skit, pretending to be campers on the first day of camp. Tara played a girl who took her blow-dryer with her everywhere.

"You mean I can't blow-dry my hair in the swimming pool?" she whined, and all the girls laughed. They knew she was teasing them.

Then Liza nudged Maddie. "Come on, let's do this," she whispered.

Crouching low, they quietly snuck away from the program and headed for the path to the boys' camp. Once they got there, they stood up straight and broke into a run.

"We've got to hurry!" Liza said. "Some of the boys might come back early."

Maddie's heart was pounding. She had never done anything like this before. It was terrifying and thrilling at the same time.

Liza made a beeline for the Charles bunk.

"Hey, that's Gabriel's bunk!" Maddie called out.

"Who cares?" Liza asked. "We need to hit as many bunks as we can!"

They slipped inside the dark bunk.

"It smells like feet in here!" Liza complained.

"Oh great. I can't wait to get to the bathroom," Maddie said.

They stepped into the boys' bathroom and Liza opened her bag. She handed Maddie a pair of thin plastic gloves.

"From the cafeteria," Liza explained. She slipped on her gloves, and then took out the jar of petroleum jelly. "All right. Ready!"

She opened the jar and took out a glob of the thick clear jelly. Then she smeared it on one of the toilet seats. Maddie started giggling uncontrollably.

"This is so gross!" she squealed.

"Shh!" Liza warned. "Come on, help. It only works if we do a whole bunch."

Maddie grabbed a glob of jelly and quickly hit the other seat. Then the girls rushed out of the bunk and ran into the next cabin. They were in the middle of pranking a third bunk when they started to hear voices coming through the woods.

"Liza, they're coming!" Maddie shrieked.

Liza stuffed the jar into her bag and nodded to Maddie. "Head for the trees!"

The girls left the cabin and raced toward the trees like spies on the run in an action movie, ducking behind buildings and rocks until they reached the woods. Then they made their way back to the quad, avoiding the path so the boys wouldn't see them.

They tumbled into the quad, laughing and gasping.

"That was awesome!" Maddie cried.

"Definitely!" Liza agreed. "One of the best camp pranks ever. The boys sit down . . . and slide right off!"

Maddie started giggling again, but the sound of Gabriel's voice made her stop. She looked up to see him sitting on the rock—their rock—with Amelia. She was laughing like Gabriel had just told the funniest joke in the world. Maddie felt a little pang in her heart.

"That's not right," Liza said. "She knows you like him."

"It's okay," Maddie said, even though she wasn't sure if she believed it. "He's not my boyfriend or anything. He can talk to whomever he wants, right?"

They both stood there for a moment, not sure what to do. For a second Maddie wondered if she should go over there, but what would she say? And what if Gabriel didn't want to talk to her?

"Come on, let's see if there are any cookies left," said Liza.

Maddie followed Liza right past Gabriel and Amelia. She waved at them, and Gabriel smiled and waved back. Amelia pretended she didn't see her.

So what if he's talking to Amelia? It doesn't matter, she told herself. But that little pang was still there, and not even a double-chocolate-chunk cookie could make it go away.

chapter 11

THE NEXT MORNING TARA CAME INTO THE BUNK FIVE
minutes earlier than usual. Libby quickly threw down her
hairbrush.

"I'm ready! I swear!" she cried.

"Relax," Tara said. "I'm just here to talk to you girls
about a prank that was played last night."

Maddie resisted the urge to look at Liza. She knew if
she did she would give everything away.

Behind her, Liza's face was a mask of innocence.
"What prank? Did the boys do something again?"

"Actually, the girls did it this time," Tara said, eyeing
her carefully. "Can you believe that someone greased the
toilet seats in three of the boys' cabins?"

Emily burst out laughing. "Awesome!"

"Ew! That is so gross!" Amelia cried, making a face.

"Anyway, Patty has asked all the counselors to

check around to see who might have done it," Tara said. "I told her that none of my Hannahs would ever do such a thing. None of you know anything about this, do you?"

Maddie struggled to look calm and cool, but she could feel the heat rising to her face. Did Tara know? Were they in trouble?

Then Amelia piped up. "Well, Liza's been saying for days that she's going to get revenge on the boys for their pranks," she said.

Liza quickly turned to Amelia and motioned texting on a cell phone, and Amelia turned pale. Liza turned back to Tara.

"Yeah, I said that," Liza admitted. "But I got salt all over my mashed potatoes. I was mad!"

"And I thought it was funny when they put my underwear on the flagpole," Emily added.

"That's just what I thought," Tara said. "All right, girls. Get ready for flag."

Tara started to walk out the door, but to Maddie's surprise she turned her head and winked.

"I don't know who did it, but it was pretty awesome," she said quietly, and then she hurried away.

Maddie fell back on her bed. Liza stormed over to Amelia's bed.

"Snitch!" Liza accused.

"Okay, chill," Amelia replied, holding up her hands. "It's no big deal. Tara's not even mad!"

Liza shook her head and walked out of the cabin. "She is the one thing I won't miss about camp," she muttered under her breath as she walked past Maddie.

Maddie jumped up and joined her friend. "That was close," she said, once they were outside.

Liza stopped and then smiled. "Yeah. But we did it," she said, and she held up her hand for a high five.

At breakfast that morning the whole camp was buzzing about the girls' prank. Jared walked over to the girls' side of the room.

"You guys think you're very funny," he said. "But I know who did it, and we will get revenge."

"What's the matter, Jared? Did you slip and slide?" one of the girls called out, and Liza and Maddie looked at each other in surprise. Their prank was a hit!

Jared just scowled and walked away.

"Do you think he knows it's us?" Maddie whispered to Liza.

"He couldn't," Liza replied, but then Maddie noticed Amelia eyeing them curiously, and she went back to eating her French toast.

When breakfast ended, Gabriel walked up as Maddie was wiping down the girls' table.

"That was a right cheeky prank last night," Gabriel said, grinning.

"Cheeky?" Maddie asked.

"Um . . . bold, I guess," Gabriel said. "But also funny."

"You're a good sport," Maddie said. She wasn't about to tell Gabriel that she and Liza had done it. Some things would always be between her and her best friend.

Then Liza nudged Maddie. "Look," she said, pointing.

Across the room, Amelia was talking to Jared. He was glancing over at their table with narrowed eyes. Maddie definitely did not trust Amelia. But what would she have to gain by ratting them out? Did Amelia like Jared now?

"Well, bye," Gabriel said with a little wave. Maddie was startled. She was so busy worrying about Amelia that she had forgotten that Gabriel was standing in front of her, trying to talk to her.

"Bye!" she said, trying not to get too flustered. "And be careful where you sit!"

Gabriel laughed and gave her a wink.

Oh no . . . did she just give herself away?

Amelia was still talking to Jared.

"So do you think she's telling him what she suspects?" Maddie whispered to Liza, who was now standing next to her, when Gabriel was out of earshot.

"Maybe," Liza replied. "But I'm not going to worry about it. Today's my last full day at camp. We need to have some fun."

The last day of the first session was also a wrap-up for most of the activities. In archery, the girls held an elimination tournament, taking turns in rounds to see if they could outshoot one another. In the end, it was Samantha against Liza, and Liza won with a shot right outside the bull's-eye.

"Nice one," Samantha complimented her, and Liza grinned.

"I'm leaving on a high note," she said.

In drama, they put on a skit that they had been practicing for the last week. The girls also wrote a play about camp counselors.

"Faster! Faster!" Maddie yelled in her role as a counselor. "You're going to miss flag!"

"But it's three o'clock in the morning!" wailed Liza, who was playing a camper. Tara laughed.

At free time, Libby asked Maddie if she wanted to practice tennis.

"It's Liza's last day," Maddie said. "But next week, we can practice all you want."

"I bet you'll be sorry you said that," Libby said mischievously.

"Thanks, Mads," Liza said.

"So, what do you want to do?" Maddie asked.

Liza didn't hesitate. "Let's swim in the lake!"

Ten minutes later the girls were wading into the cool water. A few of the other campers had the same idea, but the lake was mostly quiet. They swam to the dock and then climbed out, sitting on the edge as they let the afternoon sun warm their skin.

"I'm going to miss you, Mads," Liza said.

"Me too," Maddie replied.

They were both quiet for a moment as they gently kicked the water with their feet. Then Liza looked at her.

"I can tell you don't like talking about your dad," she said. "But if you ever need to, call me, okay? I mean, when you're out of camp and electronics aren't considered evil."

Maddie couldn't help smiling. "Thanks," she said, and then the words just came spilling out. "It's hard to talk about, you know? Back home everyone treats me different. I'm 'the girl whose dad died.' Here I just wanted to be Maddie. And it's been pretty good so far."

Liza nodded. "I get it. And maybe when you get back home things will be more normal too. People tend to forget stuff over the summer. You'll get, like, a fresh start."

That had never occurred to Maddie before. "I hope that's true," she said. "That would be nice."

"You'll have to tell me what happens with Gabriel," said Liza.

"What do you think will happen?" asked Maddie, curiously.

"Oh, I don't know," said Liza. "Maybe he'll . . . maybe . . ." She stopped. "You know what, I don't know!" Then she started to giggle.

Maddie started to giggle too. She was glad she wasn't the only one who had no idea what was supposed to happen next.

Liza nodded out to the lake. "Race you to the first buoy?"

Maddie grinned. "You're on!"

The girls dove into the water with a splash. They swam to the buoy and back. Liza's hand touched the dock just a second before Maddie's.

"Told you I was leaving on a high note!" Liza said.

At dinner, Liza ate a veggie burger with Emily. "For solidarity," she said. Then the evening program was a good-bye to all the departing campers. When it was over, Gabriel walked over to Maddie.

"Go ahead," Liza told her. "I've got to say good-bye to a bunch of people anyway."

"Thanks," Maddie said.

Gabriel smiled when he reached her. "Hullo, Maddie."

"Hul—I mean, hello," she said.

"It's okay if you copy my accent," Gabriel told her. "It happens all the time."

"Okay," Maddie replied. "Then, hullo!"

They fell into step as they walked to get their milk and cookies. Maddie's heart started doing that flip-flop thing again. Being with Gabriel felt exciting and natural at the same time.

But he was hanging out with Amelia last night, a little voice inside her said. Maddie pushed the thought aside. Gabriel was with her now, wasn't he? Dad always told her to live in the moment. Well, that's what she was going to do.

They got their milk and cookies and sat on their usual rock. Maddie had a lot of questions about London, and Gabriel answered them all. The most interesting thing she learned was that Gabriel liked to eat baked beans on toast for breakfast.

"Sorry, but that's a little weird," she said with a laugh.

"That's okay," he said. "I think the way everyone here puts ketchup on everything is weird. Seth even puts it on his scrambled eggs."

"I do too," Maddie admitted. "It's yummy."

Gabriel shook his head. "See? Weird."

They talked until it was time to head back to their bunks. When Maddie caught up to her friends, they were full of questions.

"Is Gabriel your boyfriend?" Libby asked directly. "I mean, you guys are with each other all the time."

"Well, he hasn't asked me to be his girlfriend," Maddie replied.

"But if he did, would you?" Emily asked.

"Guys!" Liza said in a warning tone.

"No, it's okay," Maddie said. "I don't mind talking

about it. I guess, it's just, I don't know. I mean, if he were my boyfriend, how would things be different? We'd still just hang out and talk, right?"

The girls were silent for a moment as they considered this.

"It would have to be different," Libby said finally. "I mean, you'd have to do everything together and stuff."

"Ew, you would not," Emily joined in. "I mean, that would be boring, wouldn't it?"

"My mom says I can't have a boyfriend until I'm sixteen," Samantha offered.

"Maybe she's onto something," Maddie said. Crushing on a boy was one thing, but having an actual boyfriend? That sounded like a lot of work. Right now, it would be nice if everything could just stay the same.

They hadn't noticed that Amelia had been sitting on her bed, listening to them. "You guys don't know what do to with a boyfriend?" she said. "That's really pathetic."

"It is *not* pathetic, Amelia," said Liza. "We just have other things that we are interested in besides boys. Well, in addition to boys."

Amelia ignored her.

"You talk to a boyfriend every day. And you text, and

e-mail. And things get assumed. Like when you have a dance or something you know that you will dance with him. You don't have to worry about him asking you because he's always your boyfriend. Seriously I cannot believe none of you have ever had a boyfriend before." She sighed and got under her covers, presumably to text again.

Maddie thought about what Amelia said as she settled in. It sounded good. The not worrying part. Because right now she was worried about pretty much everything.

chapter 12

MADDIE WOKE THE NEXT MORNING TO THE SOUND
of shrieks and squeals. She sat upright in her bed, startled.

Emily and Libby were still asleep, but the other beds were empty. Samantha came running out of the bathroom area, giggling.

"What's going on?" Maddie asked, yawning.

"Oh my gosh, it's awful!" Samantha said, still giggling.

"Then why are you laughing?" Maddie asked.

"It's just—it's that—oh, I can't!" And then Samantha flopped down on her bed, trying to smother her laughter in a pillow.

Maddie jumped out of bed and ran into the bathroom. Both Liza and Amelia were standing in front of the mirrors, wrapped in towels and still dripping from the shower. They both looked like they were in shock, and it was easy to see why: Liza's blond hair was now orange, and Amelia's light brown hair was streaked with bright purple!

Maddie put a hand over her mouth. "What happened?"

Amelia was too angry to reply, but Liza broke into a grin.

"I have to admit, it was brilliant," she said. "The boys pranked us. They must have put bug juice in our shampoo bottles." She leaned in closer to look at her hair.

Amelia ducked into the shower and came back with her shampoo bottle. She dumped it into the sink, and grape bug juice flowed out.

"Those idiots!" she shrieked. "There has got to be some way to get this out!"

"It happened to that girl Holly last year, and she couldn't get the color out for, like, a week," Liza reported calmly. She was clearly enjoying Amelia's freak-out.

"No way!" Amelia cried. She went back into the shower, angrily tossed her towel over the stall door, and turned on the water.

Liza shook her head. "She can try, but bug juice is pretty powerful."

"Oh Liza, I can't believe this happened on your last day. How awful!" Maddie said sympathetically.

"It's okay," Liza said with a shrug. "It actually looks kind of cool."

Liza ducked back into the stall to get dressed, and Maddie returned to the sleeping area.

"You guys might want to skip showers this morning," she told Libby, Samantha, and Emily. "Looks like the boys have sabotaged our shampoo."

"What do you mean?" Libby asked sleepily.

Then Liza emerged from the bathroom, and Libby gasped.

"That looks really cool," Emily said.

"Thanks," Liza replied.

The girls got ready for flag while Amelia stayed in the shower, fruitlessly trying to get the bug juice out of her hair. Tara entered the bunk and frowned when she heard the shower running.

"Seriously?" she asked.

"Go easy on her," Liza said, pointing to her hair. "The boys got us."

"Bug juice?" Tara asked, and Liza nodded. Tara just sighed walked into the bathroom area.

Five minutes later the girls were gathered with the other campers for flag. Liza's hair was orange but nicely dried, and Amelia's hair was purple and still dripping. She stomped over to the boys' side and poked Jared in the arm.

"You were supposed to do the other shampoos, not mine!" she hissed, loudly enough so that Maddie and Liza could hear her.

Jared just shrugged. "I couldn't remember which was yours, so I just did them all."

Maddie couldn't help smiling. "Looks like her own evil plan backfired on her."

Then Patty and Jim Lewis addressed the campers.

"As you all know, today is changeover day," Patty announced. "Today we'll be saying good-bye to some of our campers, and welcoming new ones. It's also visiting day, so all of our normal activities are on hold for today."

"Tonight at dinner we'll be handing out a new activity chart," Jim added.

"So remember, be sure to wish your old friends well, and get ready to welcome some new ones with some Camp Wimoway spirit!" Patty said.

Maddie turned to Liza. The fact that her friend was leaving was finally sinking in.

"I'm going to miss you so much," Maddie said, hugging her.

"Me too, Mads," Liza replied.

The girls all headed to breakfast, where Liza drank a giant glass of orange bug juice. They were barely finished when Liza's parents came into the mess hall, scanning the room for their daughter.

Liza spotted them first and ran up to them, nearly knocking over her mother with a hug. Maddie slowly approached them, and Liza's dad gave her a big smile.

"Maddie, look at you! You must have grown three inches!" he remarked.

"Thanks, Mr. Harry," Maddie said.

"Liza, what did you do to your hair?" Mrs. Harry shrieked, when Liza let her go.

The girls told Liza's parents the whole story as they packed up all of Liza's things. It seemed to Maddie that it took no time at all before Liza was ready to go home.

Libby and Emily joined them as they carried Liza's bags to her car. Liza hugged each one of them good-bye. When she got to Maddie, she whispered in her ear. "Let me know what happens with Gabriel," she said.

Maddie felt herself blush a little and nodded.

Liza got into the car and waved good-bye as the car

pulled out. Maddie, Libby, and Emily waved and waved until the car was out of sight.

Maddie suddenly felt supersad. It would probably be a whole year before she saw Liza again.

Libby and Emily linked elbows with her.

"Come on," Libby said. "Let's get ready for our visitors."

chapter 13

BACK IN THE BUNK, THEY FOUND SAMANTHA ON THE porch, next to her packed-up bags.

"Oh my gosh, I totally forgot you were leaving too!" Maddie cried, hugging her. She had been so focused on Liza that she forgot that she would miss other people too.

"That's okay," Samantha said.

"Well, I didn't forget," Emily said. She ran inside the bunk and came back out with a small box wrapped in purple tissue paper. She handed it to Samantha. "Open it!"

Samantha obeyed and took out a handmade necklace with the words CAMP WIMOWAY spelled out in alphabet beads.

"I love it!" Samantha cried, giving Emily a warm hug. "I will never forget you guys. And I will definitely be back next summer."

They said good-bye to Samantha and went inside the bunk, where Amelia was packing her bags.

"I thought you were staying all summer!" Maddie said.

"I am," Amelia replied, sounding defensive. "I'm just moving over to the Sarah bunk. No offense or anything. But those girls are a little older and, um . . . well, more experienced with things."

Maddie, Libby, and Emily exchanged glances.

"No offense taken," Maddie answered. "You made friends with those girls pretty fast."

Amelia softened a bit. "Yeah, right. Well, I'll see you guys around."

She zipped up her big duffel bag, picking it up, and started trying to pick up all her other bags too.

"We'll help you," Maddie said, and Amelia nodded gratefully.

"Thanks!"

Maddie, Libby, and Emily helped Amelia carry her bags to her new bunk.

"Good riddance!" Emily said, as they dumped Amelia's bags on her new porch. They all smiled at one another. Maddie wondered whether Amelia moving to a new bunk meant she'd start focusing on the other boys' bunk, too.

She hoped so. She didn't like Amelia anywhere near Gabriel.

As they were walking back to their own cabin, they saw three girls loading their bags onto the porch.

"Oh my gosh, it's the volleyball girls!" Maddie cried, stopping in her tracks.

"The volleyball girls?" Libby asked.

"You guys have never met them," Maddie explained. "They always come for the second session. They're like, obsessed with volleyball, and they're awesome at it. They don't even take siesta or free time or anything—they're always on the volleyball court."

"That sounds intense," Emily remarked.

"Wait until you meet them," Maddie said.

They walked up to the porch toward their three new bunkmates. Each girl had her blond hair pulled back in a ponytail. One of the girls bounded down the steps toward Maddie.

"Hey, Maddie!" she said, holding up her hand for a high five.

"Hey, Ashley!" Maddie said, high-fiving her back. She nodded behind her. "This is Libby and Emily."

"Nice to meet you," Ashley said. Then she pointed to

the porch. "That's Alexis and Abigail up there."

"Wow, Triple-A," Emily remarked.

"How did you know we called ourselves that?" Ashley asked, and didn't wait for an answer. "Hey, after we put our stuff away we're going for a run. Want to come?"

"Well, our parents will be here soon," Maddie answered.

"I don't run," Emily said flatly. "Unless someone is chasing me."

"L-O-L!" Ashley said. "Well, catch you guys later."

Libby shook her head as Ashley, Alexis, and Abigail brought their stuff inside the cabin.

"You were right," she said. "They are intense!"

Then they heard the beep of a horn, and Maddie turned to see a car pull up to the bunk—her grandma's car!

"Grandma!" Maddie yelled, practically leaping off the porch. She ran to the car. Her mom hadn't said anything about Grandma coming on visiting day.

The car doors opened, and her grandmother, grandfather, and mother all got out. Maddie didn't know who to hug first, she was so happy to see all of them. But Maddie's grandmother ran up and hugged her first.

"Surprise!" she said, squeezing Maddie tightly. Her

grandmother was a small, thin, woman with brown hair streaked with gray, and Maddie was always surprised at how strong her hugs were.

"Save some for me," her grandpa said in his deep voice. He was twice as tall as Maddie's grandma, and he had to lean way over to hug her.

When Maddie finally escaped the hug, her mom was waiting for her.

"You didn't tell me!" Maddie accused.

"Then it wouldn't have been a surprise," her mom said. She let go of Maddie and looked in her face. "You look beautiful! I missed that face."

"I missed yours, too," Maddie said. She turned to her grandparents. "I'm glad you guys drove. I was worried she was going to end up in California or something. You should have seen her on the ride over."

"Hey, I got us here," her mom said, pretending to sound hurt.

The sound of the lunch bell rang across the camp.

"We should get to the mess hall," Maddie said.

Mom grinned and pulled a small cooler from the back seat. "I packed us a lunch. All your favorites. I figured you'd need a break from camp food."

Maddie smiled. "I know where we can eat. Let me get a blanket."

A few minutes later they were under the shade of a tree at the edge of the soccer meadow, setting up lunch picnic-style.

"I got you a chicken Caesar sandwich from Eddie's deli," Mrs. Jacobs said, handing Maddie a wrapped sandwich. "And there's that potato salad you like. And a giant chocolate-chip cookie."

"Yum!" Maddie said, happily unwrapping her sandwich. She took a bite and closed her eyes, savoring it. "This is soooo much better than camp food."

Things were quiet for a little while as everyone ate, but before long Maddie's mom and grandparents were asking her a million questions.

"How are Liza and Libby and Emily?"

"What's your favorite activity?"

"Were there any good pranks this year?"

Maddie answered everything, leaving out the part about the greased toilet seats. When they were done eating, Grandpa stood up and stretched.

"How about giving us a tour?" he asked. "I've always heard a lot about this place, but I've never seen it."

"Sure," Maddie said.

They put the cooler back in the car and Maddie led them on a tour, taking them to the mess hall, the lake, and the arts and crafts cabin. Then they headed over to the tennis courts. Maddie was dying to tell her mom about the special lessons she'd been getting from Libby, but she wanted to keep that a secret for now.

Mom's not the only one who can pull off a surprise, she told herself.

They were walking across the courts when Maddie spotted Gabriel and his mom coming toward them.

"Hi!" Gabriel called out, and Maddie felt herself turning bright red. She wasn't exactly sure why. What was the big deal?

She heard her grandfather let out a chuckle, and saw her grandmother poke him in the ribs. Maddie wished she could sink into the court, but she felt like she should say something.

"So, guess you're on a tour too," she said.

"Right," Gabriel replied, and he seemed a little uncomfortable too. His mom was giving him a weird smile. Maddie knew she probably should have introduced her mom and grandparents, but her feet had a mind of their own. She hurried off the court.

"See you later," she said, barely looking at him.

"Right," Gabriel said again.

"Well," her mom said, as soon as they were off the court. "Is that someone special?"

"Mom!" Maddie cried, embarrassed. *"No!* He's just Gabriel. He's my friend."

"Okay, okay," her mom said. "Just asking. Now let's go see the horses. Have you done any riding yet?"

"Not yet," Maddie replied. "I was saving that for this session."

Maddie continued the tour, thankful that nobody mentioned Gabriel. Before she knew it, it was time for the visitors to leave. Maddie reluctantly walked them back to the car.

Her mom grabbed her in a hug that lasted so long Maddie wasn't sure if her mom would ever let go. When she finally did, she asked, "You're having fun, right?"

"Yes," Maddie replied, and she realized she meant it—and that surprised her a little. Fun. A few months ago she thought she would never have fun again.

Mrs. Jacobs looked relieved. "I'm so glad, honey. You have a good time the next few weeks. I miss you, but you'll be home before you know it."

She squeezed Maddie again and then slipped into the backseat. Grandpa gave her a hug next, and then finally it was Grandma's turn.

"You okay, sweetheart?" she asked, looking into Maddie's eyes.

The question didn't annoy Maddie as much as it would have a few weeks ago.

"I'm good, Grandma," she replied. She was thoughtful for a moment. "How's Mom?"

"Oh, she's doing fine," Grandma replied. "Don't you worry about her. Once we got her through the first week she was much better."

Maddie was confused. "What do you mean?"

"She missed you so much, pumpkin," Grandma explained. "She didn't want you to go to camp, let alone the whole summer. She was worried she'd miss you too much, and she was worried how you'd do away from home. But your dad insisted that you go this year. He knew how much you love camp and he wanted you to have a wonderful summer doing fun things. I think he knew it would be hard at home, and he wanted you here instead."

Maddie was quiet as she absorbed all this. All along,

she had thought Mom just couldn't handle her being around. She had no idea that Mom didn't want her to go to camp. She started to think about her mom all alone in the house, and she suddenly felt bad.

"Mom isn't too lonely?" she asked her grandmother.

"Oh, don't you worry," Grandma replied. "She's had so many visitors, and all of her friends are keeping her busy. In the car up here, she was joking that she wanted everyone to stop asking if she was okay and leave her alone for a few days."

Maddie smiled. She knew just how Mom felt. "Thanks, Grandma."

Then she walked over to her mom's window and leaned inside.

"I miss you, Mom o' Mine," she said, using a nick-name from when she was a kid. "But I'm having fun. See you soon!"

Maddie's mom broke into a smile. "That's just what I wanted to hear."

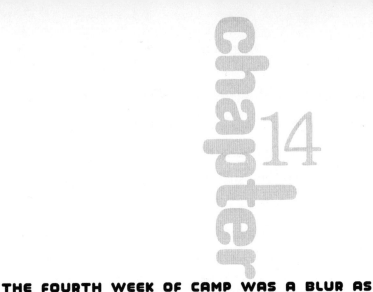

chapter 14

THE FOURTH WEEK OF CAMP WAS A BLUR AS
Maddie got used to her new activities and new bunkmates.
She had to catch glimpses of Gabriel around camp, but
she felt like she hadn't seen him in weeks. Actually the
girls in her bunk hadn't really talked that much about boys
at all. Ashley, Alexis, and Abigail woke up early every
morning, but not to shower and do their hair—they woke
up to run. They cared way more about sports than boys.
It was kind of nice. Maddie and her friends picked their
new schedules and avoided taking volleyball.

"All those girls do is spike it," Maddie warned her
friends. "It gets frustrating."

Instead, they filled their activity slots with horseback
riding, rope climbing, photography, and ceramics.
Actually, Maddie and Libby signed up for rope climbing, but Emily managed to convince the counselors to

let her take another round of arts and crafts.

Emily also managed to make some changes in the dining hall. A few days into week four, the dining hall served tacos with a fixings bar. Emily showed up at the table with two tacos.

"What, no veggie burger?" Maddie asked.

Emily grinned. "It's a tofu taco. Mrs. Hancock really liked the apron I made her. She's adding veggie chili to the menu, too, and I got her to do mac and cheese three times a week."

Maddie shook her head. "Emily, you are on a roll."

Every night after the evening program, Maddie and Gabriel met at "their rock," as Maddie liked to think of it, and talked. Some of the new girls looked at them curiously and walked away whispering, but Maddie ignored them. She and Gabriel were just talking.

One night, when she got back to the cabin, she found all of her bunkmates on the porch. Ashley, Alexis, and Abigail were not playing volleyball, for once, and they seemed to be in a chatty mood.

"We saw you with that British guy," Ashley said as soon as Maddie walked up the steps.

"He's so cute!" said Abigail.

"Is he your boyfriend?" asked Alexis.

Maddie tried not to let the question upset her. "No, he's not," she said. "We're friends. I don't see what the big deal is about having a boyfriend."

"I have a boyfriend."

Maddie turned with surprise at the sound of Emily's voice. "You what?"

Emily nodded calmly. "Yeah, Seth. I figured you knew."

Libby gave her a playful shove. "We did *not* know. When? How?"

Emily gave a pleased little smile and ran into the cabin. "Hold on."

Maddie and Libby looked at each other curiously. Emily emerged a few seconds later with—well, something Maddie couldn't quite make out.

"He made me this," Emily said, holding up the object. "It's a papier-mâché sculpture of my head."

As soon as she said it, Maddie realized that's what it was. Seth must have used a volleyball to mold the papier-mâché, because Emily's head was really round. He had made her hair out of curled pieces of paper and even made glasses out of wire.

"That is so cool!" Maddie exclaimed.

"I'd like to serve that over a net," Ashley said with a giggle, and Emily protectively held the head closer to her. "Just kidding! Just kidding! It's cool!"

"He gave me this two days ago and asked me to be his girlfriend," Emily explained. "How could I say no? I mean, he made a sculpture of my head."

Libby nodded. "It's a little creepy, but you've got a point."

"Wow. So he just came right out and asked you?" Maddie said. She was still trying to wrap her head around the whole thing. Emily, who never cared about blow-drying her hair and always had paint on her face, had a boyfriend? But why not? She was funny and cute and sweet. It had just always seemed like she didn't care about stuff like that.

"Yeah, he just asked me," Emily replied. "It's cool. He's nice. And we like a lot of the same stuff."

"Well, um, congratulations," Maddie said.

Ashley, Alexis, and Abigail filed into the cabin and high-fived Emily on their way in.

"Yeah, nice job," Ashley said.

Emily followed them in, smiling, leaving Libby and Maddie on the porch.

"You know, I'm sure Gabriel will ask you soon," Libby said.

"Maybe," Maddie said, a little crossly. Why hadn't Gabriel asked her? Did it mean he didn't like her? "Whatever." And then she walked into the cabin, leaving Libby behind.

The next morning, Maddie woke up in a bad mood. It wasn't that she wasn't happy for Emily; she just couldn't shake the feeling that there must be something wrong with her and Gabriel.

At free time that afternoon, Maddie flopped down on her bed. Libby came up and grabbed her by the arm.

"Oh, no, Miss Maddie," she said. "Now that we don't have tennis every day, we need to practice whenever we can."

Maddie reluctantly got up. Even though she didn't feel like it, she knew Libby was right, and she really wanted to surprise her mom. When they got to the tennis courts, Libby had some new advice for Maddie.

"You know, I've been thinking that maybe you're trying too hard," Libby said. "My instructor always tells me to take some deep breaths before a game. When you're relaxed, it's easier to get into the rhythm."

"The rhythm of what?" Maddie asked.

"Of the ball," Libby said. "Come on, close your eyes and take three deep breaths."

Maddie felt silly, but she tried it.

"Okay," Libby said. "Now keep your eye on the ball, and feel the rhythm. Don't worry about anything else. Not even beautiful Gabriel," she teased.

Maddie flushed hotly. But she took Libby's advice and just concentrated on the yellow ball.

Libby gently lobbed the ball over the net, and Maddie swatted it back right to her. Libby returned it, and Maddie hit it back again. They hit the ball back and forth a few more times before Maddie missed it.

"Rats!" she cried, but Libby was encouraging.

"That was great!" she said. "You're getting it, Maddie!"

For the first time, Maddie felt like she might actually figure out tennis after all.

Now if I can only figure out this thing with Gabriel, everything will be great! she thought.

chapter 15

THE NEXT WEEK BEGAN WITH ANOTHER ALL-CAMP activity on the lake. Once again Maddie hurried to try to get a kayak, but they were all gone by the time the arrived. Then she spotted Gabriel waving to her by a canoe. Maddie ran over.

"I tried to save us kayaks, but those three volleyball girls are really fast," he reported. "They grabbed the last ones."

Maddie laughed. "That's Ashley, Alexis, and Abigail. I call them the volleyball girls too. But thanks for getting us a canoe."

"I thought it might be fun," Gabriel said, and the two of them grabbed onto the canoe and dragged it into the lake. Then Gabriel waved his arm toward the canoe. "After you, my lady," he said.

"Why, thank you," Maddie replied, and she climbed aboard.

Soon they were paddling across the lake. It was another beautiful day, with birds swooping and soaring in the blue sky overhead.

"I can't believe there are only two more weeks of camp," Gabriel said. "Then I have to start school." He shuddered.

"I kind of like school," Maddie admitted. "But if I had a choice, I'd rather stay at camp."

"I'm rather worried that American school will be different from school in London," he said. "What's it like here?"

"Well, you're going into seventh grade, right?" Maddie asked.

"I think so," Gabriel replied. "They name the years a little bit differently. Is that the same as middle school?"

Maddie nodded. "Yeah. And we have different subjects, like math and reading and science and social studies and computers. And a foreign language. And then there are usually electives, like sewing and woodworking and stuff."

"What about PE?" Gabriel asked.

Maddie frowned. "PE?"

"Physical education," Gabriel answered.

"Oh yeah," Maddie said with a nod. "We call that gym. Yeah, we do that every day. But there's no rowing, like at your old school."

Things were quiet for a moment, and Maddie noticed that they were all the way in the middle of the lake. Gabriel frowned.

"We've lost the current," he said. "See how still the water is? It's going to take us forever to get back."

And what would be so wrong with that? Maddie thought.

"Just wait," Maddie said out loud. "My dad taught me a lot about the water when we used to go boating together. Sometimes you just have to sit still and wait to see what the current or the wind will do. Then you'll know which way to go."

They sat quietly for a few minutes, waiting and looking around the beautiful lake. It was quiet and peaceful and Maddie felt okay not saying anything, just sitting there with Gabriel. She wasn't even thinking that there were only two weeks left for him to ask her to be his girlfriend. Well, she wasn't thinking about it too much. Then, sure enough, the water began to ripple, and a little breeze began to blow.

"Paddle left," Maddie instructed, and soon they were paddling with the current and moving swiftly back to shore.

"Your dad must be really smart!" Gabriel remarked.

"He is," Maddie replied. Then she realized what she'd said. She still was never sure what tense to use. "Well, I mean, he was."

Gabriel looked at her questioningly, and Maddie decided there was no use keeping it from him anymore.

"My dad died last fall," she said. "He was sick for, like, a year, and then it looked like he was getting better, and then he got really sick again, really fast." Her eyes started to tear up, remembering.

Gabriel was tearing up too. "Oh, I'm so sorry."

"Thank you," she said.

And then they just kept paddling. Gabriel didn't ask any more questions or say anything to try to make her feel better, and Maddie was grateful.

At the sound of the counselor's whistle they brought the canoe back to shore.

"Thanks for telling me, Maddie," Gabriel said when they climbed out of the boat. "I really am sorry about your dad."

Then he hugged her. At first, Maddie thought she

might faint. She stood there for a second with her arms at her sides.

Hug him back! a little voice inside her urged, and she cautiously returned the hug. Gabriel smelled like sun and water and summer.

The hug lasted maybe five seconds, but when it was done Maddie felt like she was tingling from head to toe.

"Um, thanks," she said shyly. "See you later."

Gabriel smiled and waved to her as she headed back to the bunk—and it felt like she was floating the whole way. She knew she had to get ready for her next activity, but after she changed out of her swimsuit she took out one of the flower cards she and Liza had made together.

Dear Liza, she wrote. *You will not believe what just happened . . .*

chapter 16

MADDIE COULDN'T STOP THINKING ABOUT THE HUG
all day. At lunch, she waved to Gabriel as he walked back
to his table with his tray, and he waved back. Part of
her wanted to go up to him and say something, but she
stopped herself. That wasn't their thing. They ate meals
separately, and then hung out during downtime. She
didn't want to rock the boat.

Rock the boat. Just thinking about the canoe brought
back that tingly feeling she got from the hug. She realized
she must have been smiling because Emily quizzed her
when she sat down.

"What's up, Maddie? Are you as happy about the mac
and cheese as I am?" she asked.

"Um, yeah," Maddie lied. She wasn't ready to tell
anyone else about that hug yet. "Gotta love that mac and
cheese."

But at dinner that night, neither Maddie nor Emily were smiling—but for different reasons.

"Mac and cheese again?" Emily asked. "I mean, I love it, but twice in one day?"

"Be careful what you wish for," Libby quipped. "At least, that's what my grandma always says."

Emily sighed and poked at her macaroni and cheese with her fork.

But Maddie wasn't paying attention. Her eyes were focused across the mess hall, where Amelia had planted herself next to Gabriel, at a boys' table! Not only that, but she and Gabriel were talking and laughing. Maddie felt jealous, and then wondered if she had a right to. He wasn't her boyfriend—but what about that hug?

During the evening program that night, the counselors led the campers in a game of flashlight tag. It wasn't super dark out yet, but the flashlights made it more fun. But Maddie couldn't really get into the game, because she kept watching Gabriel. Just like at dinner, Amelia planted herself right by his side, running after him and chasing him.

So Maddie was relieved when the game was over and

Gabriel walked right to her, just like he always did.

"All that running has me famished," he said. "I might need two cookies."

They got their milk and cookies and then sat on their rock, talking more about school. Gabriel still seemed nervous about it. Maddie was relieved that Amelia didn't try to hang out and talk with them.

When downtime was over, Maddie and Gabriel stood up. She looked at him expectantly, hoping for another hug, but he just gave his usual wave.

"Night, Maddie," he said as he walked away.

"Night," Maddie replied, feeling deflated.

Back in the bunk, Maddie flopped down on her bed.

"What gives, Maddie?" asked Ashley, who now had Liza's old bed. "You look down."

Libby walked over and sat on the edge of Maddie's bed. "Is it because of Gabriel hanging out with Amelia? I saw them at dinner."

"No! I mean yes. I mean . . . I don't know!" Maddie cried, putting her pillow over her face.

"Whoa. This thing with the British dude sounds complicated," Ashley said, and Maddie removed the pillow and sat up.

"It is complicated," she confessed as Emily, Alexis, and Abigail moved in closer, listening intently. "This morning he hugged me. And then he's hanging with Amelia? And at downtime he acted like everything was the same as before. Aaargh!"

She flopped down again.

"Wow, he hugged you?" Libby asked. "Maddie, he must *so* like you."

Emily nodded. "I haven't even hugged Seth, and he's my boyfriend."

"So what does that mean?" Maddie asked. "He's your boyfriend. How is that different from when you were just friends?"

Emily shrugged. "I don't know. It's just different."

"But Gabriel isn't your boyfriend, so you just want to know if he likes you, right?" Ashley asked.

Maddie nodded.

"So let's look at the facts," Ashley said in her matter-of-fact way. "Does he talk to you?"

"Yes," Maddie answered.

"When you're with other people, or do you hang out and talk alone?" she asked.

"Mostly alone," Maddie replied.

"And he hugged you?"

Maddie nodded again.

"That settles it," Ashley said firmly. "He likes you."

Alexis and Abigail were shaking their heads.

"That's not enough," Alexis piped up. "He has to do something special for you."

Emily nodded. "Right. Like give you a papier-mâché head."

Maddie made a face. "Um, I don't think he knows how to make a papier-mâché head."

"Then he could make it out of clay," Emily suggested.

"I think what Emily and Alexis are trying to say is that if he really likes you, he'll ask you to do something special with him, like go out for ice cream or something," Libby interpreted.

"But he always gets me a cookie at downtime," Maddie pointed out. "And anyway, it's not like you can go out for ice cream at camp."

"I think it's clear that he likes her," Ashley said. "And so what if he's not her boyfriend? They can still like each other, right?"

"He has to make it clear," Abigail chimed in. "He has to do something cool, like what Seth did for Emily."

"I really do not need a papier-mâché model of my head," Maddie protested.

"You know what she means," Libby said. "I think he does like you. But maybe he likes Amelia too. So you need to be sure."

"Exactly," Maddie said. "But how?"

"The ball's in his court," Libby replied. "It's his serve."

Maddie stuck out her tongue. "Please don't make this about tennis."

"Just wait and see," Emily suggested. "I bet he'll do something. I have a feeling."

Maddie sighed. "Whatever he does, I hope it happens before camp is over!"

chapter 17

AS MADDIE DRIFTED OFF TO SLEEP, SHE KEPT thinking of the hug and wondering what it meant.

He probably just felt bad for me when he heard my dad died, she convinced herself. *The hug didn't mean anything more than that.*

And then, unexpectedly, her grandmother's voice popped into her head.

Your dad wanted you to have a wonderful summer doing fun things.

Maddie's dad knew how much she loved camp. He wanted her to have fun—and she was, except when she was trying to figure out the whole Gabriel thing.

I will keep having fun, she promised herself. *And I won't ruin it by thinking about Gabriel all the time!*

Not thinking about Gabriel all the time wasn't easy, but as the week progressed, Maddie found herself getting into a rhythm, just like on the tennis court. She fell in love with Apple, the chestnut-brown horse she was assigned in her horseback-riding class. Even though she was more comfortable in the water than on a horse, she quickly got the hang of Apple's gentle trot.

In photography, she took shot after shot of the lake, trying to capture the water as it rippled in the breeze. In ceramics, she painted a beautiful vase in her mom's favorite colors, red and green. And in rope climbing, she tried her best to get through the rope course. A series of ropes crisscrossed a small field, leading to obstacles to climb over. The object of the activity was to learn how to get through the course, and Maddie knew it wasn't going to be easy. Libby, on the other hand, scrambled up the obstacle walls as if she was defying gravity.

"It's my tennis training," Libby would say, playfully showing off her biceps when Maddie would ask her how she did it. "Just another reason to keep playing, Maddie."

And every night, she and Gabriel still met at downtime. They talked about boating and school and American TV shows and music, and every night Maddie secretly hoped she'd get another hug, but it never came.

After downtime, Maddie would head back to the bunk to find Tara on the porch, reading with a flashlight as she waited for the girls to get home.

"Did they ask you to double-check on us or something?" Maddie asked one night. "I mean, you always used to check on us *after* curfew."

"No, it's just that my friend Lara—you know, one of the swim instructors?" Tara began, and Maddie nodded. "Well, she had to leave camp early this year and I miss her. We used to hang out at downtime, but not anymore. So here I am. It stinks because I can't even text her or call her."

"Yeah, that does stink," Maddie agreed. "I miss Liza a lot too. But I've been writing her letters."

"She's lucky to have you as a friend, Maddie," Tara said.

"Thanks," Maddie said. "And we're lucky to have you for a counselor."

Tara smiled. "Thanks."

Before Maddie knew it, the last week of camp began. Week six was always exciting and sad at the same time. The Lewises always did something really special for the evening programs. Monday night it was a movie under the stars, and curfew was extended by an hour so everyone could watch.

Maddie grabbed her blanket and headed to watch the movie with Libby and Emily.

"I hope it's not a scary movie," Libby said with a worried expression on her face.

"They're never scary," Maddie promised. "In fact, it's usually like a boring little kid movie with talking animals or something because they don't want the little kids to get scared. But it's still fun because it's outside."

When they got there, Gabriel was waving her over, motioning to the rain poncho he had spread out on the grass. Maddie turned to her friends.

"Do you guys mind?" she asked.

"Not at all," Libby said, taking the blanket from her. "Have fun!"

Maddie felt nervous as she walked over to Gabriel.

"I saved you a spot," he said, sitting down on the poncho. Then he motioned for her to join him.

Is this the "something special" I've been waiting for? Maddie wondered, and her palms immediately got sweaty. Normally Gabriel would sit with his friends during the evening program, but they were nowhere in sight.

She scanned the crowd and saw Seth and Scott from Gabriel's bunk sitting next to Emily and Libby.

Okay, so maybe it's not a big deal, she told herself. *Maybe the boys are just mixing it up.*

But she couldn't shake that awkward feeling.

Patty Lewis appeared in front of the crowd. "Welcome to movie night, campers!" she announced in her game-show-host voice. "We've been getting requests to do something a little spookier on movie night, so we've switched things up a little bit. So tonight prepare to enjoy . . . *My Uncle's a Werewolf!*"

Most campers clapped, and a couple groaned.

"Poor Libby! She didn't want to see a scary movie," Maddie said, looking over at her friend, who was hiding her face in her sweatshirt.

"I saw it on the plane," Gabriel said. "It's a kid's movie. Not too scary."

The crowd quieted down as the movie started, and Maddie soon learned that Gabriel was right. The film was pretty tame, but in one scene, the kids in the movie are walking through the woods at night, slowly, and then suddenly . . .

"Aaaaah!" Maddie shrieked, along with half the

campers, as a werewolf jumped out of the shadows in the film. Instinctively, she reached out and grabbed Gabriel's arm. He looked down at her and smiled.

Flustered, Maddie pulled her arm back. Gabriel looked over and smiled at her, but that only made her feel more awkward. She put her hands in her lap, but that got uncomfortable after a while. She shifted and sat cross-legged, planting her palms at her sides, but then Gabriel shifted and his left hand brushed against her right hand, so she quickly moved it.

Maddie pulled her knees up to her chest and wrapped her arms around them. That worked—for a while. Even though it was a chilly night, she couldn't seem to stop sweating. She tried leaning back with her arms planted in the ground behind her, and that worked pretty well. Just when she thought she needed a new position, the movie, thankfully, ended.

They stood up and stretched, and Gabriel looked at his watch. "We've still got twenty minutes before curfew. Want to go for a walk?"

Maddie panicked, her mind racing. This was it. This meant he definitely liked her. Maybe he was going to ask her to be his girlfriend.

Yikes! She had been dreaming about a moment like this for days, and now that it was right in front of her, something in her gut didn't feel ready.

"Um, I have . . . a stomachache," she said awkwardly, backing away from him. "I should go back to the bunk."

Gabriel looked concerned. "Let me walk you back."

"No thanks," Maddie said quickly, and then she turned and practically ran off, leaving a very confused Gabriel standing there, holding his poncho.

What just happened? Maddie asked herself as she quickly slipped into her pajamas in the bunk. *I mean, I wanted him to like me. I think I even wanted to be his girlfriend. And then he did just what I wanted, and it felt good . . . and scary at the same time.*

Maddie got under the covers and pretended to be asleep. She knew her friends would have a lot of questions when they got back, and she didn't feel like answering them. So she closed her eyes, feeling bad about the way she ran off on Gabriel, but cozy and safe at the same time.

I'm sure it's okay, she told herself. *I bet everything will still be the same tomorrow.*

chapter 18

BUT MADDIE SOON FOUND OUT THAT THINGS weren't the same. The next night the counselors put together a fun game show for the evening program. It was a camp tradition. They set up the mess hall to look like a game show stage, with a glittery paper sign strung across the salad bar that read CAMP WIMOWAY TRIVIA BLOWOUT!

Alyssa, the counselor who taught the drama class, was the emcee.

"It's bunk against bunk in the most intense trivia challenge in Camp Wimoway history!" she announced. "Who will win?"

The campers let out a wild cheer, and Maddie scanned the crowd to see if she could find Gabriel. He was usually pretty easy to spot because he was so tall. She finally found him leaning against a table, staring straight ahead. He didn't look for her and give her a wave like he usually did.

"All right, let's get this game rolling!" Alyssa announced. "Hannah bunk and Betty bunk, come on down!"

Maddie forgot about Gabriel and ran up to the stage area with the other Hannahs. She loved trivia night, and she was usually pretty good at it. The Hannahs and the Bettys faced off against one another, with Alyssa in between them.

"First question goes to the Bettys," Alyssa asked. "How many dapple gray horses are in the stable?"

The girls whispered to each other and then one answered, "Two."

"Correct!" Alyssa cheered. "Hannahs, it's your turn. What color flip-flops does your counselor, Tara, wear?"

The girls huddled together.

"I think they're blue," Maddie said.

"That sounds right," Ashley agreed.

"Are you sure they're not green?" Libby asked.

"Definitely blue," Emily offered.

Maddie turned to Alyssa. "Blue," she said.

Alyssa grinned. "Correct!"

The game went back and forth until the Bettys got a question wrong. Then the next bunks were called up from the boys' camp.

The Hannahs kept winning. Finally, it was down to the Hannahs and the Rickys, the bunk that Brandon and Jared were in.

"They're going to be tough to beat," Maddie whispered to her teammates. "Brandon and Jared have been going to this camp since they could walk."

The mess hall got crazy as the girls cheered, "Hannahs! Hannahs! Hannahs!" and the boys cheered "Rickys! Rickys! Rickys!"

Alyssa had a question for the Rickys. "How many yellow kayaks are at the lake?"

The boys whispered to each other as the other campers chanted. Finally Brandon answered. "Three?"

"Wrong!' Alyssa said. "Hannahs, if you girls get this you will be the Camp Wimoway Trivia Champions!"

Libby frowned. "I almost never go near the lake. I don't know."

Maddie closed her eyes. "I think I've got it," she said, picturing the lakeshore in her mind. There were the kayaks, lined up as always. One green one, one yellow one, one blue one, another green one, another yellow one . . ."

Her eyes flew open. "Two!"

"Is that your final answer?" Alyssa asked.

Maddie nodded. "Yes. Definitely two."

"Correct! The Hannahs win!"

The mess hall erupted in applause and cheers (and a few boos from some of the boys). Maddie jumped up and down and Libby and Emily, and Ashley, Alexis, and Abigail high-fived everyone.

When the excitement died down, Maddie scanned the crowd for Gabriel, but she didn't spot him. She checked the cookie line, but he wasn't there. Then she headed out to their usual rock, but Gabriel wasn't there, either.

That's weird, she thought. She waited by the rock for a few minutes, but then started to feel awkward, so she headed back to the bunk. Tara was on the porch steps.

"Good job tonight," she said. "You're back early!"

Maddie just nodded and walked inside. She didn't mean to be rude, but an awful feeling was welling up inside her. What if Gabriel didn't like her anymore?

She got ready for bed and tried to sleep, but her mind was racing. She hadn't noticed Amelia during downtime, either. Were Amelia and Gabriel together? The thought left a lump in her throat.

The next day, she was sure something was up with Gabriel. They never spent much time together during the day, but he had stopped his friendly waving. And that night, he did another disappearing act at downtime. The evening program was a glow-stick party outside, where the campers listened to music and made swirly light patterns in the air. Gabriel stayed with the boys the whole time, and afterward, when Maddie went to look for him, he was nowhere to be found. *This is bad*, thought Maddie. *Really bad.* Camp was ending in just a couple of days. And unlike for Liza, it didn't look like it was going to end on a high note for Maddie.

Once again, Maddie headed back to the bunk early. Tara was there as usual, and this time she patted a spot on the step next to her. Maddie sat down and leaned against her shoulder.

"Boy stuff?" Tara asked.

"Maybe," Maddie replied cautiously. "I'm not sure." She felt silly talking about it, but Tara was so nice, like a big sister. "It's just that, Gabriel and I are friends, and we sat next to each other during the movie, and I think he likes me and stuff, but then he asked me to go for a walk and I freaked out a little and just left him standing there."

She let out a deep breath. It felt good to get all that

out. She glanced at Tara, worried that Tara might think she was silly, but Tara looked thoughtful.

"Well, do you like Gabriel maybe as a boyfriend?" Tara asked.

"Yes!" Maddie replied without hesitating. It was the first time she felt sure. "But, well . . . I don't know. I like thinking about him. I like the idea of him. But the idea of actually having him as a boyfriend is kind of, well, kind of scary."

Tara let out an understanding laugh. "It's okay," she said. "Sometimes boys are a lot better from a distance. You can like a boy and not do anything about it."

"You can?" Maddie asked. She had never considered this before.

Tara nodded. "Sure! That's what a crush is all about. You don't even have to let the boy know about it if you don't want to."

Maddie thought about this. "You know what's weird? The whole time I was worried if he liked me or not. I wonder if he was worrying if I liked him. I never did say anything."

"And you don't have to say anything until you're ready," Tara said. "But it's not good to hurt someone's feelings. Gabriel is probably wondering what he did to make you run off like that. He might be avoiding you because he's embarrassed. It would be really nice if you could talk to him."

Maddie stomach lurched. "What would I say?" she asked. She couldn't imagine having that conversation with him. *I was afraid to be your girlfriend so I ran. Awkward!*

Tara thought for a bit. "You'll figure it out," she said. "Just treat him the way you would want him to treat you."

Then she stood up. "Now go on in and make your bed before you get in it," she said. "I didn't dock you today on the chores list, and I won't as long as it's done by bedtime!"

Maddie smiled. "Yes, chief!" she said, saluting.

Maddie went inside and neatly pulled up her sheets. She lifted up her pillow to fluff it, and her dad's note slid out from under the pillowcase. Maddie sat on the bed, turning it over in her fingers.

Nobody else was back yet, the bunk was quiet, and camp was almost over. Maybe now was the time. She unfolded it and began to read.

Dear Madeline,

I hope you are having a great time at camp. Are you still boating a lot? I'll bet you are such a great boater this summer. Be sure to get out on the lake as much as possible.

The world will change and go by plenty fast outside of camp, but inside all I want you to do this summer is have fun and enjoy it. Paddle slowly. Listen to the water. Look up at the sky. Feel the sun on your back. Be still, and when the current changes and when you feel the wind on you, you'll be ready and know which way to point your boat.

You have great instincts, Mads, on the water and on land. I know that whatever you do will be the right thing when you trust your gut. I'll be thinking of you always, Mads. I love you forever and a day . . . keep rowing your boat merrily along . . .

Love,
Dad

Maddie's throat was tight. She folded up the letter and carefully slipped it back underneath her pillowcase. It was just like Dad to tell her exactly what she needed to hear at the exact right time.

I like Gabriel, Maddie thought. *I really do. But I haven't felt the wind or the current yet, and I'm not sure, just yet, which way I want to row.*

chapter 19

"WE ARE THE CAMPERS OF CAMP WIMOWAY,

You can't catch us 'cause we will swim away,
We run and craft and play games every day,
We are the campers of Camp Wimoway!"

The campers' voices rose together as they sang the camp theme song. Around them, the smell of sizzling hot dogs and burgers filled the early evening air as the campers and counselors gathered outside to celebrate the last night of camp. Jim Lewis helped Mrs. Hancock grill burgers on a giant outdoor grill, while some campers roasted their hot dogs on sticks over the fire pits.

"I will never get tired of that song," Emily said as she, Libby, and Maddie carried their food to the nearest empty picnic table.

"It's ridiculous, but it's catchy," Libby admitted.

Maddie nodded. "Sometimes at home, I sing it in the shower," she confessed, and her friends burst out laughing.

They sat down, and Emily bit into her burger. Maddie raised an eyebrow.

"Emily, is that a veggie burger?" she asked.

Emily nodded. "Number thirty-one. I have to admit, I kind of missed them."

"I can't believe this is our last night," Maddie said, looking out at the velvet blue sky, where the first stars of the night were starting to appear. "It went so fast. I don't want to go back!"

"I don't know," Libby said. "I mean, this was my first year coming for the whole summer. I kind of miss home."

Emily nodded. "Me too. My mom said she recorded all fourteen episodes of *Ultimate Craft Challenge* for me. I miss TV!"

"But I don't get to see you guys for a whole year," Maddie pointed out.

"But we have technology at home," Emily pointed out. "We can text and do a video chat."

"Oh my gosh, what a good idea!" Libby squealed. "We have to tell Liza. Then the four of us could get together whenever we want. Sort of. You know what I mean!"

Maddie grinned. "Yeah, that would be nice."

Emily stood up. "I need another veggie burger!" she

announced, and then marched off to get one.

"What about you, Maddie?" Libby asked. "Another hot dog?"

"I'm full," Maddie replied. She was actually more nervous than full. Tara had given her good advice, but every time she started to approach Gabriel since then, she had chickened out. Tonight was her last chance. But first she had something to say to Libby.

"Thanks for the tennis lessons," she said. "That was really nice of you. I know you could have played with someone a lot better than me. But I really appreciate the help."

"It was fun," Libby replied. "Plus, you're sooo much better than you were at the beginning of the summer. Your mom's going to love it."

Maddie got a little pang at the mention of her mom. Maybe she did want to go home after all.

Then she spotted Gabriel a few tables away, sitting with Brandon, Jared, and Scott. She had been waiting to feel the current, as her dad would say, to know which way to go, and now she finally felt it. She took a deep breath. "I'll be back. There's something I've got to do."

Libby raised an eyebrow, but didn't ask any questions

as Maddie got up and walked over to Gabriel's table.

"Hi, Gabriel," she said, her heart racing. "Can I talk to you a minute?"

Brandon and Jared smirked.

"Go say good-bye to your girlfriend," Jared teased, giving Gabriel a nudge, and Maddie saw Gabriel blush a little. He got up and they took a few steps away from the table.

"I wanted to apologize for the other night," Maddie said quickly, before her courage left her. "I didn't really know what to do or how to act. This year has been full of changes for me and next year will be too and right now . . . well, right now I just need things to stay the same for a little bit. I'm sorry if I acted like a crazy person."

Gabriel smiled. "You didn't act like a crazy person," he said. They stared at each other for a moment. Then finally Gabriel spoke again. "I'm not sure what to do, either, Maddie. I like you, but there are quite a few changes in my life too. I'm nervous about camp ending and starting a new school and living so far away from my dad. And, you know, the whole living in a new country thing. Actually a new continent."

They both laughed. "Well, welcome to your new

continent!" said Maddie. "Changes are hard. I get it. And I'm sorry if I hurt your feelings the other night. When we stopped meeting at downtime I figured I'd really messed up."

"I thought that's what you wanted," Gabriel said.

Maddie shook her head. "Not really," she said. "I like hanging out with you. And I'm glad we talked about it before camp ended. I can't believe it's over already." They were both quiet. Maddie realized that she wouldn't see Gabriel for a whole year. That was weird. Would he be different next summer? And if so, how? Better? Worse? What if he turned into a jerk? Or what if she didn't think he was cute anymore? Maddie stole a sidelong glance at him. No, she would definitely still think he was cute.

"Can I text you after camp?" Gabriel asked suddenly.

Maddie beamed. "Of course! I can help you if you have any questions about school in the states, or well, with anything else."

"Excellent," Gabriel said, smiling.

He leaned in for a hug, and Maddie didn't back away. Her stomach did a flip-flop, but it was a fun one. Instead of feeling confused and anxious, she felt excited.

Hug number two! I can't wait to tell Libby and

Emily, she thought. *And I've got to write to Liza!*

"So do you think you'll be back next summer?" Gabriel asked as they broke off the hug.

"Definitely!" Maddie answered. "For the whole summer!"

"Well then, I guess I'll see you next summer, Madeline," Gabriel said, his eyes twinkling.

Maddie giggled. "See you next summer, Gabriel. Good night."

She watched him walk back to boys' camp and every few steps he turned around and waved. She giggled and waved back. Next summer seemed so far away.

She stepped away and walked off, staring up at the beautiful sky. A bright white star was twinkling right over-head, and Maddie made her wish.

I wish that I can always remember how I'm feeling at this very moment right now.

And then she rolled back to the bunk . . . merrily.

ANGELA DARLING was nicknamed "The Love Guru" by her friends in school because she always gave such awesome advice on crushes. And Angela's own first crush worked out pretty well . . . they have been married for almost ten years now! When Angela isn't busy watching romantic comedies, reading romance novels, or dreaming up new stories, she works as an editor in New York City. She knows deep down that *every* story can't possibly have a happy ending, but the incurable romantic in her can't help but always look for the silver lining in every cloud.

Here's a sneak peek at the next book in the series:

Lindsay likes Nick.

CR♥SH

Does he like her too?

Lindsay's Surprise Crush

"DID YOU HEAR WHAT HAPPENED TO NICK LOPEZ?"

A tingle rippled up and down Lindsay Potter's spine. She stared at her friend Rosie. "No! What? What happened to him?" she asked.

"You'll never believe it," said Rosie, lowering her voice to a whisper. Then she glanced at someone over Lindsay's shoulder. "Oh! Look! Sasha got her hair cut!"

Lindsay turned, trying not to show her frustration, and smiled and waved at Sasha, who was just stepping off her bus to join the throngs of kids milling around and socializing on the first day of school. She turned back to Rosie, trying to keep her voice even and not sound too anxious. "*What* happened to Nick?"

"Oh! Right. Nick. Well, I heard from Chloe, who heard from Jenn, that he . . ."

"Move along, girls, the bell's going to ring any

minute," said Mr. Drakely, the teacher on morning bus duty. He was herding middle schoolers in the direction of the main school entrance. Sure enough, the bell rang a moment later.

"See you fourth period!" called Rosie, hustling up the steps, her new purple backpack bouncing on her back.

Lindsay's thoughts were swirling as she made her way quickly to her locker. She knew just where it was—she'd had the same one last year, her first year of middle school. She spun the dial for her combination and wondered if anyone had managed to fix the sticky door over the summer. One yank told her no one had. Sigh. Another year with a sticking locker door.

Twang! The locker finally decided to open. She smooshed a few things into it and slammed it closed again, eager to get to homeroom to find out what had happened to Nick.

Nick was her best friend. They'd been babies together. Actually, their friendship was even older than that. Their moms had met in pregnant-lady-exercise class!

How could she not know what major catastrophe had happened to her best friend? True, they hadn't seen each other since June. She'd gone off to visit her cousins in

Cleveland for a week, and when she'd gotten back, he was already gone—first to baseball camp, then soccer camp, then some other kind of jock camp way out in the wilds of Maine, near where his dad lived. And when he finally returned, she had been gone again, first to music camp, and then driving her older brother up to college to help him move in.

Maybe Nick had broken his leg or something! She frowned. Maybe whatever had happened to him was the reason he hadn't returned her texts last night. She'd texted him twice, once to tell him they were in the same homeroom, and then again to ask him if he'd heard the rumor that Mr. Bates assigned homework to his home-room students. And he hadn't responded. Was he in the hospital? In traction? No, he would have been able to text if he were in traction. Maybe both his hands were bandaged with second degree burns or something? She swallowed uneasily. What a way to start seventh grade.

She walked into Mr. Bates's homeroom. The second bell had not yet rung, so kids were wandering around, chatting, hugging long-lost friends, and complimenting haircuts and new sneakers. She looked around the room quickly, trying to spot Nick. He wasn't there. Maybe something truly terrible had happened to him!

She saw Jenn, who waved her over toward the desks near the window. She also saw some really tall new guy who was surrounded by kids. He seemed to try to catch her eye, but she looked away quickly. She could feel the worry creeping over her.

"Hey, did you see Nick?" a voice whispered from her right side.

She turned. It was Sasha.

"No!" she said. "Where is he?"

Sasha pointed quickly with her finger. A tiny giggle escaped her.

Lindsay followed her gaze. Her brow furrowed. What was Sasha talking about? She seemed to be pointing toward that new kid. He was a head taller than all the other kids in the room. He looked tall enough to be in high school. Was he standing in front of Nick? Lindsay craned her neck to get a better look. The new kid had really dark hair and broad, muscular shoulders. He looked really cute from behind. And then he turned around. He . . .

. . . *was* Nick.